Nancee Cain

Serrated Edge Publishing

ဢ Praise for *Saving Evangeline* ဢ

"*Saving Evangeline* has stayed in my head for the better part of a week. I think the possibilities it opens up and thoughts it inspired is a testament to Nancee Cain's storytelling."

ဢ *The Literary Gossip Blog*

Six-Star Review and 2015 Top Pick: "I laughed my butt off and cried my heart out. I swooned with the passion and felt warm & fuzzy with each hug. This book touched me in so many ways. When a book does that I give it 6 Stars without question."

ဢ*Smut Book Junkies Blog*

"I forgot how to breathe; this book completely swept me off my feet. I will remember it always. By the time I got to the end of this book it felt like a prayer. Beneath the beautiful imagery, the religious figures, the humor, the sadness, is an epic love story. A 6 star read!"

ဢ*After This Page Book Blog*

"If you're looking for a story that is BEAUTIFUL and yet so REAL, *Saving Evangeline* is it. It has the perfect amount of depth and humor. It'll keep your attention and it will captivate you."

ဢ*Beauty in the Beastly Books Blog*

Five Stars: "This story had such a unique feel to it and was brilliantly written. It was hilariously funny and incredibly addictive."

ဢ*Totally Booked Blog*

In the Top Ten list for 2015.

ဢ*Kat Loves Books, A Booklover's Blog*

✑ Praise for *Tempting Jo* ✑

"Ladies and gentleman, Nancee Cain does it again! I just LOVE the way she writes about angels and make them seem so human."

✑*Beauty in the Beastly Books Blog*

"…her stories really make you feel genuine emotions. At first I was half in-lust with Luc and I can totally understand Jo's fascination with him, but Rafe…oh brother! I want my own guardian angel and he must be just like him!!"

✑*Kat Loves Books Blog*

"*Tempting Jo* is a battle between Heaven and Hell, good versus evil with a human caught in the crossfires. This is a book you want to finish in one sitting even if it's 7am, because you just have to know what happens between these characters."

✑*Southern Book Nerd Blog*

"Nancee Cain creates magic in the pages she writes: her angels are sinfully unangelic, her humans are downright flawed and completely relatable, her plots are impeccable, and her writing is genius."

✑*Paranormal, Magic & Mischief Blog*

Serrated Edge Publishing
PO Box 969
Jasper, AL 35502
www.nanceecain.com

First published by Love Kissed Books in the anthology *Haunted By Love*,
August 2017

Chapters one and two of *Tempting Jo*, copyright © 2016

Cover Design for *The Resurrection of Dylan McAthie* and
The Redemption of Emma Devine by Shannon Lumetta

ISBN: 978-0-9976139-6-4

10 9 8 7 6 5 4 3 2 1

Editor: Katherine Pace
Cover Photographer: Chantell Reid
Cover Model: Wendy Hinckle
Cover Design and Book Design: Coreen Montagna

Printed in the United States of America

For all the Cain Raisers
who begged for Luc's story.

CHAPTER ONE

Ennui — A feeling of listlessness and dissatisfaction arising from a lack of occupation or excitement.

I tear the page off Jo's Word-a-Day calendar and fashion it into a paper football. Today's word couldn't be more appropriate. I switch the television off the news. I'm sick of it. Another war. The stock market is down. Jobs are non-existent. No one is happy with the government. A no-talent, wannabe star is posting on social media, and hate is rampant in the world.

Big fuckin' deal.

Nothing holds my interest these days. One day of chaos blends seamlessly into another. It's monotonous, and I don't deal well with boredom. The last time I had any real fun was six months ago. Tempting Jo held my attention for a while, but as usual, things went per His plan, not mine. And to make matters worse, not only am I out a human toy, I'm down a decent administrative assistant in a business I couldn't care less about. I've been through seven since Jolene Sanford left.

Thankfully, this chapter of my life will end tomorrow when the new owner of the company takes over. In baseball terms, I'm like a pinch hitter. Every so often, The Boss has me stir shit up on Earth.

Truth be told, it's a PR stunt. I do the dirty work, and He looks great. I'm long overdue a vacation, and right now this sorry planet is self-destructing without my help. Those imbecile humans are doing my job for me.

From the big screen television, a televangelist cries and begs for money. Disgusted, I frown and turn away. Sometimes high definition isn't that great. Who wants to see sweat and nose hairs?

"The end is near! Satan is amongst us and we must battle evil! Fighting evil is expensive, but with your generous contribution, the Devil can be defeated. Dig deep, give until it hurts, do it for the Lord," he wails.

I roll my eyes. The only thing that will hurt is some old woman's bank account while that rich bastard lives the good life. Hell, that asshole's Rolex is worth more than mine. Not that I need a new watch. Time means nothing to me. The past five hundred years are a blur of repetitiveness. Sure, the technology has changed, but let's face it, hate is hate.

"Lucifer is rampant, we must rally against evil. Together, we shall overcome, and your donation will help spread the message to sinners everywhere…" The pompous ass mops his brow as he paces back and forth. Why don't the humans understand his true, underlying message? He needs to pay for his private jet, his mistress's plastic surgery, and the new Hawaiian home he purchased to keep his wife's mouth shut. He doesn't give a shit about sinners.

Me, on the other hand, I *love* sinners.

Let me introduce myself.

I'm Lucifer, but you can call me Luc DeVille.

My office door opens just as I flick the paper football, and it hits my office manager on the forehead. Mrs. Cabot steps back, shaking. With her beady eyes and pale face, she always looks like a scared rabbit. Dammit, I miss Jo's gumption. She was the best administrative assistant I ever had.

Irritated by my own moodiness where Jolene Sanford is concerned, I'm shorter than usual with my haggard secretary. "What?"

"S-Sorry to interrupt, but your ten o'clock appointment is h-here. I guess you didn't hear me knock, sir. You t-told me to usher her in straightaway. My apologies, sir." Her gray corkscrew curls bob with her nervousness. While I love subservience, I prefer it in the bedroom with a side of sass.

"Fine." I stand and straighten my red tie.

Tired of being vilified for every horrible thing that has ever happened, I've decided to write a tell-all book. It's about time folks heard my side of the story.

The words flowed, and *Give the Devil His Due* was completed in a mere four weeks. Anticipating at least a six-figure advance, I submitted it to the big five publishers and waited for the bidding war. I had no doubt it was a masterpiece, destined to put Dante's *Inferno* to shame.

To my surprise, every damn one turned it down, citing it as an unimaginative work of fiction. I strongly suspect The Boss had something to do with this. It's a brilliant story. And it isn't *fiction*. It's an apologist's view of evil: my life story. Not to be outwitted, I have a plan to sidestep His interference. I've decided to go indie and self-publish.

I forgot today is my appointment with a top New York editor to assist me in the process. I hope she has some guts and isn't some sniveling namby-pamby human. It wouldn't hurt if she were easy on the eyes, either...

A familiar fragrance precedes my guest into the office, the unmistakable scent of *her*. I've lived forever, and not much surprises me, but this? It fucking blindsides me. My eyes drink in the statuesque beauty walking toward me. Her sleeveless black dress hugs her generous curves to perfection. It's too low-cut and an inch too short to be deemed appropriate work attire.

Not that I mind. Not one bit. But, what in Heaven's name is *she* doing here?

A well-manicured hand reaches out and firmly grips mine. I'd wince, but I'll be damned if I give her the upper hand this early in the game. Aware of our audience, I motion Lili to have a seat. Dismissing Mrs. Cabot with a nod, I watch the nosy old woman scurry out the door, leaving me alone with my past.

Rattled, I bark, "What are *you* doing here?"

Lili gracefully folds into the chair and smiles. "Haven't you heard? Lilith Nix is the most sought after editor in New York."

"Maybe I should move to London," I mutter, crossing my arms and leaning against my desk. "I hired BBB, the Biblio Book Bitch."

Her soft laughter both entices and irritates me. It always has.

"I'm shocked. This isn't like you to not do your homework. That would be me, Samael. Can't we let bygone be bygones?"

Only Lili still goads me by calling me by this name. It's one of my many less popular names, and I dropped it thousands of years ago. "I go by Luc, now. Or, *sir*." I wink at her.

"Sir? In your dreams." She giggles and pats her professionally styled red bun. "Luke? Like the gospel? That's hilarious. Why are you using the doc's name? He's so sanctimonious."

"No, L-U-C," I stress through gritted teeth. "Where have you been?"

I hate her hair pulled up like that. I like it wild and free, especially after a night of hot, raunchy sex, or wrapped in my fist as I smack her ass.

She leans back and crosses those smooth, endless legs. I hope for a *Basic Instinct* peek, but she's classier than that, dammit. I sit behind my desk, not wanting to risk embarrassing myself like some horny teenaged human. Lili's always had this effect on me—actually, on *all* males, no matter the species. Even my demonic beast, Black Shuck, rolls over for a belly rub when she's around.

I move my stapler and sort my paperclips by size. "I've changed my mind. I don't think I want to pursue a writing career after all."

Steepling her hands, she gazes at me. Flames flicker in the depths of those intense blue-green eyes. "You disappoint me."

"Ah, well, it wouldn't be the first time, would it?"

"True." Lili picks up her purse and stands. "I just didn't figure you to be a coward. Tell me something. Are you scared of the story you have to tell, or me?"

"Scared?" I laugh. "I'm not *scared*. I don't know that you're qualified—"

Before I can finish my sentence, she leans across my desk and slaps a résumé on my desk. I know I should be looking at her face, but the view of those tits rising and falling have my full attention.

"I'm *overqualified*, numb nuts. I just wanted to see if you had the balls to work with me. I guess I have my answer."

Her stilettos click across the floor and her sexy ass sways, beckoning me like a siren's song. Damn that woman always could get under my skin. Life with her was never boring, that's for sure. I wait until her hand is on the doorknob.

"I didn't know you were still interested in my balls, love."

She glances over her shoulder and smiles. The room sizzles and snaps with sexual energy. It's always been this way between us. Our lovemaking is hot and nasty; our fights are downright brutal and dirty.

"Love?" The frostiness in her voice makes the a/c seem like a furnace. "Your assistant knows how to reach me. The proverbial *ball* is in your court. My fee goes up for every hour you make me wait on your decision. As you know, I don't like wasting time."

"Duly noted. I have all the time and money in the world. I'll review your résumé, and if it suits my *needs*, I'll be in touch."

"Touching won't be part of the agreement." She opens the door.

"I do so love a challenge," I reply with a small chuckle, just to irritate her.

The door slams behind her, and I laugh. In the space of fifteen minutes, life has taken an interesting turn. I prop my feet on my desk and bide my time.

"Ass," I hiss under my breath, slamming his door.

The old lady who escorted me into Luc's office jumps. "I-Is there anything I can do, Ms. Nix?"

"Put arsenic in his coffee?"

Her mouth drops and she swallows, visibly nervous.

"I'm returning to New York. Your boss knows how to reach me." I walk away without a backward glance.

Stepping in the elevator, I take a deep breath, furious. I'm madder at myself than at that handsome devil. Even after all these years, and all we've been through, Luc still makes my heart race and breath catch.

I hate him.

I love him.

We cycle through this every few years. It's like there's a centripetal force pulling us back together, no matter how hard we try to stay apart. The canned music overhead plays Adele's "Hello." Coincidence? I doubt it. I tap my foot. What had I been thinking? Deep down in my troubled psyche, I must be a masochist to put myself through this.

But his letter of inquiry had intrigued me. A tell-all autobiography? The last time Luc crossed the line with The Boss, he was banned from Heaven. I don't want to think about what will happen this time…It would be prudent on my part to back away from this project. However, I'm not known for being cautious. And, to be totally honest, my female pride wanted to see if Luc knew he'd sent the letter to *me*.

The elevator doors open revealing a woman holding a crying baby. My anger escalates in direct correlation to the increased pitch of the child's wailing. Everyone shifts to make room for them.

Unable to stand the ear-piercing screams one second longer, I punch the door closed and snap, "Put a plug in its mouth and shut that kid up."

The young mother attempts to soothe the child as a man nervously adjusts his necktie and glares at me. An older woman and two flibbertigibbets whisper harsh admonishments before cooing at the annoying wailer. I ignore them. Their opinions mean nothing to me. When the doors open, I elbow my way out, not caring that I'm being a rude bitch. I wish I could erase the entire last hour of my long life.

Outside the air is hot, heavy, and still, but at least I can now breathe. I need to get away. A vacation would be nice, someplace beautiful, where I can be alone to think. I pull out my phone to book a flight and find a text:

You're hired.

My heart soars and immediately plummets. Here we go. Round whatever. The sex will be incredible, the break up vicious. After seeing Luc again, I decide I'm just not up for it. Feeling like the coward I accused him of being, I text back:

Too late. I'm on vacation.

I wait, but there's no answer.

I can't decide if I'm happy or disappointed.

CHAPTER TWO

It took me all of five minutes to track Lilith down. Angelic GPS, I guess you'd call it. Or the fact she's my soul mate, even if she doesn't want to acknowledge it. However, I took my time getting here. After all, I can't have her thinking I'm desperate, or anything. It's been three weeks since she appeared out of nowhere at my office.

The house is secluded and unseen from the road. A security gate blocks the entrance, but I easily crack the keypad code and enter. It's like driving through a lush, tropical paradise. Who knew Florida had anything this nice? When I think of Florida, I think college spring break, biker rallies, and annoying family vacations at Mouse Hell.

I cut the engine and wonder if she's expecting me. *Probably.* Our relationship resembles the tide, sometimes gentle, other times crashing, but always constant. Stepping out of the car, I breathe in the salt-laden air. Black Shuck bounds after me, and I whisper for him to sit. A breeze rustles the palm trees and Royal Poincianas surrounding the small, modern house. Overhead, seagulls squawk and the rhythmic pounding of the surf mixes with music drifting from behind the house. Taking the rock path, I find a vision more glorious than the waterfront view. She's lying on her stomach, sunbathing by the pool.

Kneeling beside my naked beauty, I kiss my favorite freckle on her warm shoulder. She tastes of salt and suntan lotion. This creature is mine. Always has been, always will be.

"You're too fair to be lying in the sun," I murmur, pushing her red ponytail aside to nuzzle her neck.

"It took you long enough to get here." She sighs. "Now go away, I'm on vacation."

"What a coincidence, so am I. We can make it a working vacation." I lick the shell of her ear, and her soft whimper lets me know this isn't a lost cause. "Give in to it, darling."

Lili sits up, covering herself with a brightly colored floral beach towel. *What a pity, I love those tits.* Sunglasses hide the fire I'm sure blazes in her pupils.

"You know I'm not wired that way. Now leave."

"Yes, so your first lover whined, *ad nauseum.*" I smirk. "I, on the other hand, value your independent nature."

She thinks she's dismissed me. We both know I'm not going anywhere. This is part of the game. I shove my hands in my pockets and grin, loving the reaction I've provoked. Lili is a beautiful angel on any given day, but when angry, she's super hot.

The sun ignites the fire of her red hair as it blows in the warm breeze. Picking up a bottle of water, she downs it. Only this magnificent being can make such a mundane move sexy as hell. I can think of something else I'd like between those full lips.

"This is insane. We keep repeating the same mistakes over and over." Lili stands facing me, clutching her towel tight.

"So maybe we need to try something different?" Using her towel, I pull her closer and kiss the tip of her freckled nose.

She pulls her sunglasses down a notch and glares at me. "So far, I don't see anything different. You're trying to seduce me."

"Is it working?"

Her chin lifts. "No."

"See? Something different." I smack her towel-covered bottom. "Now get dressed, we have work to do."

"Work?"

"Work," I affirm.

"Where are you staying?" Her voice holds a hint of hope and suspicion.

And she hasn't said no. *Perfect.*

"Here, of course."

"I didn't invite you. It's a small house."

"Even better," I purr. "Besides, all the hotels on the island are booked and very few take pets. Holiday weekend and all that shit. Hip, hip hooray for the USA."

"Fine. The guest room is clean." She flounces off, looking smug.

"Guest room?" *This isn't quite what I planned.*

She pauses at the sliding glass door leading into the house. "Or you can sleep on the beach with the sand fleas, makes no difference to me."

"Guest room it is." I chuckle retrieving my suitcase as Black Shuck roams and does his business. Lili may have won this battle. But the war is far from over. We're destined to be together. She knows it. I know it. We just have to make it through the fighting and not give up this time. That's the uncharted territory in our relationship.

But this I do know.

It will happen.

I will conquer my ex.

And she'll damn well enjoy it.

That insufferable ass. It's the last in a long list of names I've called him as the hot water turns cold. I hope Luc—with a hard *k*—wants a shower, and it's cold. He hates anything cold…

Holy crap! That's it!

I smile and do a victory dance. *Why haven't I thought of this before?* I know how to get rid of him and protect my heart. I'll be cold and aloof. An ice princess! Squeaky clean, I step from the shower and lotion up my sun-tinged skin. Luc's right, someone with my coloring can't be in the sun for long. I think at least a million more freckles have popped out.

Dressed in shorts and a sloppy T-shirt, I forgo makeup and yank my hair into a messy bun. Taking a deep breath, I stare at myself in the mirror. *You can do this, Lili. Just stay strong in the face of overwhelming temptation. Do* NOT *fall for his smooth seduction and lies.* I smile as I head toward the kitchen, confident in my plan.

A loud bark and the clacking of claws skittering across the tile floors alert me to the impending attack. Using the doorframe, I brace myself for the two hundred pounds of black demon hound lunging toward me.

"Hey, boy. How are you?" I withstand the wet, sloppy kisses on my cheek and scratch behind his ears. Terrifying in looks, I love this dark beast, nonetheless.

"Black Shuck, sit."

Immediately the fiend sits, wagging his tail with impatience, his tongue hanging between ferocious-looking canines. Most creatures do what Luc commands, *especially humans.* Look up the word *charisma* and you'll probably see his picture.

I give the hound from hell another pat on the head, attempting to ignore the magnetic pull of his owner's blue eyes. They aren't a cold blue; they're warm, like the center of a burning match, and they've always had the ability to see right through me.

Luc collapses on the sofa, stretching his long legs onto my coffee table. He's dressed in jeans and a starched white shirt with the sleeves rolled up, the epitome of casual elegance. "Where's Nahash?" He's one of the few that didn't find my Burmese python intimidating.

"She died ten years ago."

"I'm sorry."

I nod, knowing his sympathy is sincere. He's like that. He lulls you into a false sense of security before doing a one-eighty and turning into a complete ass.

He opens his laptop. "So how does this work? Do you edit by hand or computer?"

With those mesmerizing blue eyes and blond hair, he's seriously hot, and I'm parched in more ways than one. I retreat to the kitchen to pull myself together and grab a cold bottle of water from the fridge. Returning, I offer it to him, but he declines with a shake of his head and a frown.

"You know better. It's cold, which is disgusting."

I laugh. I do, but I love tormenting him.

"I typically use track changes on your document. Email it to me." I rattle off my email and take a seat in the chair.

"You can sit next to me. I don't bite." He pats the couch.

"Liar. You do, too."

"And you love it."

He's right, I do. It's hard to be cold and aloof when Luc is in a playful mood. There's nothing I'd love more than to curl up next to him and just talk. For too long I've felt off and restless. Not being of this world, yet being in this world is a lonely experience. Luc is one of the few who understands the uniqueness of my situation.

But we never just talk. We have mind-blowing, wild sex and then we argue over trivial shit, slinging words meant to hurt and then we part, vowing to never see each other again.

Opening my laptop, my mail program dings, signaling the arrival of his autobiography. I open the document and begin reading. I inwardly groan at the cliché title. Keeping my face neutral, I scan the first chapter.

"It's great, right? Those publishers don't know what they're talking about. It wouldn't surprise me if The Boss hasn't had some influence in getting this blocked. But, I'm going to beat Him. He's out of touch. Authors can now control their own destiny through self-publishing." Luc leans forward. Cocky anticipation crosses his face. "Well?"

I have no idea what to say. Luc usually succeeds in everything he does. If his talent doesn't get a job done, his bullshit will. But this drivel sounds like the opening for an episode of *The Twilight Zone*.

I hit a few keys, hit send and watch his face light up as he opens the document. In a moment, his brows pull together and fire rages in the depths of his eyes. The force of his anger is so strong it knocks the power off. In a moment, the hum of the generator starts and the lights come back on.

I sigh and place a call to report the outage and hang up. "A temper tantrum? Really?"

"You wiped my story and send back a message saying, '*It sucked.*' What did you expect?" he roars. He crosses his arms and if I'm not mistaken, he's pouting.

I shrug. "You're not the first person to think they can write. Just accept the fact that this is not your thing."

Luc leaps to his feet, pacing. His fiery wings expand and flap with his agitation.

"Stay away from the curtains if you're going to throw a fit."

His wings fold and disappear. "He got to you, didn't He? The Boss told you to do this, right? He doesn't want me exposing Him—"

"Don't be ridiculous. You know I'm not one of His favorites."

"That's about the only thing we have in common besides terrific sex," he mutters.

"Eh, I've had better," I lie, examining my cuticles.

He stops in his tracks. "I beg your pardon?" The ice dripping from his voice is in direct contrast to the fire burning in his eyes. The room temperature skyrockets. He's one pissed off angel.

I stand and face him, enjoying his flustered state. "Hungry?"

His eyes narrow. "For?"

"Food. Spaghetti to be exact."

"What restaurant?" His shoulders relax and the temperature in the room drops.

I smile. Like any typical male, food is one of the keys to his heart. "No restaurant, I'm cooking."

"Uh, I don't mind taking us out to eat..." The pained look on his face is funny, if insulting.

"I'll have you know, I'm a great cook."

"Since when? Last I remember, you couldn't boil water."

"Since cooking shows became popular on television. And besides, I had you around to boil the water. Now if you're done throwing shade on my culinary skills, I'll go start supper. Why don't you take a walk?"

"Is this your polite way of telling me to go take a hike?" he asks with a captivating, boyish grin. That look has melted many hearts, mine included.

I laugh in response. "Who? Me?"

He teasingly shakes his finger. "Yes, you. And you won't get off that easy. I'm here to stay until my book is done. It might behoove you to get to work. Unless of course, you want me here."

"*Behoove* is an antiquated term. That's part of the problem with your book. You need to connect with today's reader, not their dead great-grandparents."

I've missed his wit and snarky attitude, so like my own. No one ever got me the way he does. No one has ever loved me the way he did. What I must remember, is no one has ever devastated me the way he has. I shore my flagging resolve. *Calm, cool, and collected.* That will be my mantra.

"I suggest you get busy writing. I can't edit a blank page."

He swears under his breath as I head to the kitchen. Black Shuck follows me, and Luc whispers, "Traitor."

With his tongue hanging out, the beast looks like he's grinning, and I swear he winks at me. I understand Luc's hesitation regarding my cooking. This is a new hobby, but it's become my passion. And it's much safer than sex.

The back door opens, and the familiar smell of tobacco accompanies the tapping of Blind Draeke's cane.

"He's here." The grizzled old man puffs on his pipe and grunts when Black Shuck nudges him to be petted.

"Yes." I keep my voice steady. My friend may be blind, but his other senses are keen and in tune to every unseen nuance.

"Not surprised," he responds, chuckling. He pets Black Shuck earning the hound's undying devotion.

"I don't find it amusing." I chop the tomatoes with more force than needed.

"You two cycle back together almost like clockwork. Why don't you just make a go of it and quit fighting it?"

Why, indeed? "I'm not discussing my personal life with you."

"She thinks I'm bad for her." Luc leans against the doorframe, his arms crossed. "She's right of course, but bad can be good." He smirks.

"And bad can be bad. I like to think I've learned from my past mistakes."

I wash my hands, ignoring my audience. The fragrance of fresh tomatoes, basil, and garlic permeates the air, and I stir the simmering sauce.

"That smells great." Luc inhales and peers in the pot.

I slap his hand away before he dips a finger in the sauce.

"That's hot!"

"Why thank you, glad you noticed."

"The sauce, not you."

"My girl's turned into a right good cook," Blind Draeke responds, grinning. "If you stick around, you'll be fat like me. Why don't you two just kiss and make up? You know it's inevitable."

I walk by and pat the old man's grizzled cheek. "Don't forget about free will—now butt out and quit acting like a *shadchan*. We're not acting out *Fiddler on the Roof.*"

Luc's gaze follows me as I pull salad makings from the refrigerator. For spite, I bend over a little more than necessary, wiggling my butt just a bit. I bite my lip to keep from laughing outright when I hear Luc's ragged deep breath.

"I think I'll go for that walk." The back door slams behind him.

I giggle and Blind Draeke shakes his head. "Someday you two will listen to me and quit playing games. I'm going back to my place."

"You're not staying for supper? You were actually invited, unlike some."

"I think you're a little too old to need a chaperone."

"True, we're more likely to need a referee."

"Not if you two learned to play nice. Being stubborn doesn't keep you warm at night."

"Good thing it's summer." I hug him a little longer than usual. "I wish you'd stay."

"I know you do. Trust me, this is for your own good." Chuckling, he pats my cheek.

"I do trust you. It's him I don't trust. I'll bring you some supper when it's ready."

He taps his way out the back door toward his small bungalow next door. I don't remember a time when Blind Draeke hasn't been in my life. He's the closest thing to a parent I've ever known. His only annoying quality is playing matchmaker anytime Luc's around.

I hate to disappoint my friend, but it isn't going to work. I plan to maintain a professional relationship with Luc.

I know I'm lying to myself.

But I don't know what else to do.

CHAPTER THREE

I drum my nails on the counter. Supper is ready, but Luc hasn't returned. My heart sinks a little at the thought he might have left for good.

Appetite gone, I pack Blind Draeke's meal for delivery and walk next door, hoping to find Luc there. He isn't. The knowing smirk on my old friend's face annoys me, and I kick myself all the way back home.

I should be relieved he's gone. Ecstatic even. But I'm neither. Nor am I the least bit hungry. I blink back tears. This is ridiculous. I hate criers. I'm *not* a crier; it's a sign of weakness. If I were human I'd blame it on hormones. I'm not, so I'm confused by my uncharacteristic show of emotion. Instead, I pour myself a glass of wine and head out back to nurse whatever the hell this is.

Disappointment?

Anger?

Sorrow?

All of the above?

A cool breeze makes the sultry air bearable. I walk past the pool and head down the boardwalk toward the gazebo. It's my favorite place to think. The lanterns are lit, and although I slow my pace, my heart races and I smile. Luc stands with his back to me, watching the pounding surf.

Fool, here you go again.

A gull squawks and soars above us. Without turning around, Luc comments, "Is there any lonelier sound than the call of a seagull?"

I stand next to him, watching the sun sink into the water amidst a sky awash with orange, yellow, and pink. The bird flies after his partner. "Gulls aren't lonely. They mate for life."

"Maybe that's where we went wrong." He smiles and takes a sip of my wine.

I gaze at his lips, longing to taste them and mentally shake myself.

"Look, we were never *right*. Let's just accept that it wasn't meant to be and move on. We can at least be friends." *I hope I sound more convincing to him than I do to myself.*

He gazes at me and a small smile teases the corners of his mouth. He raises my glass. "To friends…"

I nod and let out the breath I've been holding. Maybe he finally sees how toxic we are as lovers.

"With benefits?" The boyish, hopeful look would make me laugh if he wasn't the most infuriating angel on Earth.

"Keep the glass. Dinner is ready." I walk away, a coward at heart.

But it's my heart I'm protecting.

He follows me, whistling as if he didn't have a care in the world. Black Shuck bounds past us with a happy bark.

"Why don't we eat in the gazebo?" Luc suggests, catching up to me.

"Candlelight, a beach, and moonlight. How unoriginal. No wonder your writing is terrible." I yank the back door open, but he blocks my entrance with his arm.

"Sometimes tried and true works best." His warm breath tickles my neck.

My face heats at the recollection of many passionate nights with the same scenario. Ducking under his arm I retort, "We're eating in the kitchen. The meal is ruined anyway."

Luc closes the door and Black Shuck settles beside the kitchen counter.

"It smells hellacious."

I stir the overdone pasta. "Most people would say *divine*."

Washing his hands, he then dips his finger into the pot and tastes the simmering sauce.

"Damn, girl. You *can* cook. You know I meant hellacious in a good way. I'm not like 'most people.' I'm not human and neither are you." He grabs a piece of cold garlic bread, dips it in the sauce and chews thoughtfully. "Maybe that's what pulls us together."

"Perhaps. So, if that's the case, what drives us apart?" I blurt. Immediately, I want to kick myself for asking. *Must remain distant and cool...*

"The same damn thing." He rubs the back of his fingers down my jaw and gazes at my mouth, his thumb stroking my bottom lip. It takes everything in me not to suck on it.

Sexual electricity sparks between us like a live wire. My breath catches as he lowers his face to mine. He doesn't close his eyes, and flames flicker in their depths. Melting into the kiss, I whimper. It feels so natural, so right, and I never want it to end...

My brain slams on the brakes. My pulse pounds, my breathing sputters. I shove against him, angered by my body's betrayal.

"There's my girl, feisty as ever."

"I'm not *your girl*," I hiss, getting ice for my tea so that I can cool off in front of the freezer.

"You *are* mine and always will be."

I grit my teeth with frustration. "I'm not a pet to be owned. I won't be sitting up and begging for your love like your silly, human one-night-stands. You're almost as bad as Adam."

He flashes a wicked grin. "What if I promise not to make you beg? And let you be on top?"

I chunk a piece of ice at him. "Get out."

"And waste this delicious dinner? No way." He serves himself a heaping plate of spaghetti. Leaning against the counter, he eats, sipping the long noodles through those sensuous lips.

Every damn thing he does turn me on. I'm hopeless. And pathetic. Am I that desperate?

His grin broadens. "This is really good. Maybe television wasn't the downfall of civilization. What else can you cook? How about my favorite, devil's food cake?"

"You're impossible."

"Yes, I've heard that before." Luc's brows pull together. "Aren't you going to eat?" He shakes his head when I put ice in a glass for him. Instead, he reaches for the room temperature wine.

The glare I level at him bounces off him like light on a mirror. It has no impact, whatsoever. "I've lost my appetite. You ruined it." I hate how bitter I sound.

"I'll take that as a compliment. It must mean you still care…"

I groan inwardly. If I admit he's right, he wins. If I eat to prove him wrong, he'll know that's what I'm doing. It's a no-win situation. Just the way he likes things. He's the most frustrating being I've ever encountered.

"Your conceit has no boundaries." I busy myself wiping the spotless counter.

"I love it when you talk dirty to me." He twirls a bite of spaghetti and holds it out to me. "Come on, Lili, just one bite. Don't you want to slurp my, er…*the* noodle?"

"Ha!" But his teasing does the trick, and I reluctantly accept the fork. Why am I fighting this? It's a losing battle, and we both know it. That tiny piece of my heart that remains unbroken begs me to resist. I don't know that I'll survive when he leaves this time.

And he always leaves. His job is more important than I am.

He finishes his dinner and washes his dishes as I put away the food. Sadly, I realize this comfortable companionship is what my soul longs for.

Shoving the thought aside, I assume my business persona. "Shall we get busy on your memoirs tonight or wait until tomorrow and get a fresh start?"

"I can think of better things to do tonight…"

"Oh? A round of backgammon? Gin rummy?"

Luc scowls. "If you want to play hard to get, I'm game. Wearing down your defenses is half the fun."

I sigh, knowing he's right. He's the tide, and I'm the sand castle. Eventually, I'll crumble from his continued onslaught, but not tonight, Satan. Tonight, I'll stand firm.

Squaring my shoulders, I lift my chin. "I'm not playing. I'm done with this roller coaster ride. See you in the morning." I walk away.

I hate to admit it, but my heart sinks a little when he doesn't try to stop me.

CHAPTER FOUR

After a sleepless night of tossing and turning, I awake to the smell of coffee and stagger into the kitchen. Leaning against the doorframe, I pause to admire Luc's tan, toned back. He turns and raises his cup in greeting. His running shorts sit below the V of his hipbones. I drink in his appearance like a woman lost in the desert stumbling upon an oasis. I know from experience that happy trail is a roadmap to unequivocal pleasure. I pull my gaze back to his face. Unshaved, his blond hair tousled, he looks well-rested and gorgeous. Me, on the other hand? I tossed and turned all night. No amount of special eye cream will diminish the bags I'd seen under my eyes when I brushed my teeth.

I hate him.

I want him.

He chuckles. "What's on the agenda today? Aside from kinky sex and working on my book?"

"Kinky sex is not one of the services you are procuring. Just editing and probably ghost writing, judging by what I've read."

"My, my, aren't we touchy this morning. You need caffeine, my dear. And my writing isn't *that* bad."

I raise one eyebrow. "It reads like a pedantic textbook and put me to sleep in no time."

"Ah, that accounts for the lovely lavender circles under your eyes." His blue eyes twinkle with devilment.

"Smart ass." I gratefully accept the coffee he hands me. "Do you want breakfast?"

"Depends on what you're offering. You with some chocolate and whipped cream would be delightful."

I roll my eyes. "You're just full of clichés."

"I aim to please."

"Don't you have some clueless human you can use these pathetic pickup lines on?"

"Always." He stares out the window, not speaking for a moment. "I'm tired, Lili." His voice sounds uncharacteristically soft, his look pensive.

I put my cup down. "Tired? You can go back to bed if you'd like." I quickly add, "Alone."

"Not that kind of tired. Just…" He shrugs. "I don't know."

I stare at him, trying to stay one step ahead. I think I need more coffee before trying to figure out this angel's angle. As if reading my mind, Luc refreshes my cup, and I instinctively step back. It's eerie how well he knows me.

"I want to propose an idea."

I wait for the punch line. With Luc, nothing is ever as it seems. There are always strings attached.

"You said last night we could be friends. Could we give it a try?" His gaze holds mine.

Here we go.

"With you, being friends means benefits. Not no, but *hell no*. I'll work with you on your damn book, but that's it."

"I don't care about the book. I just want…never mind." He turns his back to me and hangs his head, his arms outstretched, gripping the counter. His fiery wings droop and disappear.

Curiosity gets the best of me. "Want what?"

He looks over his shoulder at me. "Twenty-four hours to just be with you. No hidden agenda, no games, it will be a true vacation. I just want to relax and be myself with someone who understands me."

I laugh at his preposterous proposition. "No sex. No flirting. Just hanging out together?" I laugh so hard my coffee sloshes in my mug. When he doesn't immediately respond, my laughter dies. An awkward silence lingers.

"Yep. Let's pretend we're boring humans. They seem happy enough at times. Maybe a little flirting; I'm not a monk."

"You're kidding me. You sneer and make fun of humans."

Luc nods. "I did and still do. Not many of them are worth anything, but then one comes along and surprises you."

I cock my head to the side and study him. "Did you love her? Or him?" I ask softly.

My gut clenches at the thought. I know he's not celibate; he isn't wired that way. And I'm fine with him having one-night stands, but...

He frowns and rubs his finger over the granite counter. "I don't know. I don't know that I'm capable of love. She was intriguing, for sure." He looks at me and my toes curl. "Jo reminded me a lot of you. She didn't take shit off anyone. And she truly cared about *me*."

Ah, he's talking about the human that won the heart of Raphael. I heard all about it from Madge. A tinge of jealousy zips through me, but I push it aside. I'm surprised by his self-awareness. He's right. Being incapable of love *is* his problem. And it's my problem because I *do* love him.

"So, you're proposing a truce?" I'm not one hundred percent sure I can trust him, but I want to. And he's right; it's exhausting not being able to show your true self. This is exactly what I've missed, connecting with other angels.

"Yeah. For twenty four hours. Unless you're too chicken to try."

My feathers ruffle before settling. I know what he's doing. He knows I won't back down from a challenge.

"Fine." I hold out my hand, sure he's going to either kiss it or yank me closer. At this point in time, I'd be fine with either. I'm hopeless where he's concerned.

To my surprise, he gives it a firm handshake. "Good. I'm going for a run, be thinking about what you want to do today as we explore being human." He whistles for Black Shuck, who follows his master out the door.

This strange turn in our relationship feels surreal. Twenty-four hours. As friends. It's never happened before.

I give him twelve hours to fuck it up.

Friends? *What was I thinking?* Lili and I don't do the friends thing. We fuck and we fight. And repeat the same cycle every few hundred years. In our long history together, I've never suggested such a thing. She doesn't trust me, which makes her smart and boosts her appeal.

The wind gusts and storm clouds appear on the horizon. I jog down the beach with Black Shuck trotting beside me. Ahead, a family is setting up an umbrella, and the mother worriedly eyes the dark cloud overhead as she unpacks their gear. The small boy cries, hysterically pointing at my massive beast, and his father picks him up.

"He's not going to bother you. See? The doggie's playing in the water." The ignorant bastard bounces the kid on his hip.

If he only knew. One silent command and my "doggie" would become a killer capable of destroying all three of the humans. But right now, Black Shuck barks at the waves, carefree.

Lucky bastard.

And I mean the human, not my dog. I slow to a walk, kicking the sand. Envy courses through my veins. Maybe humans don't have it so bad; that family looks happy. *Is it love? Or an unawareness of just how shitty life really is?* I remember love…yet, here I am, alone. And worse than that, *lonely* thanks to my pride…

Sensing my unease, Black Shuck bounds back toward me. He barks and wags his tail, as if he can read my thoughts, and agrees.

"Shut up, I didn't ask you." I pick up a piece of driftwood and throw it. He bounces off, happy to chase a stick. My life would be so much simpler if that's all I ever chased.

Maybe it's time to start over. New beginnings, making amends, and all that shit. I can look at this as a self-challenge. Like fasting, it will improve my mindset and help me once again focus on my actual job of portraying evil. Thunder booms as lightning zips across the sky.

I glare at the heavens. Okay, so I've never lasted more than eight hours fasting, He doesn't have to be catty about it. The heavens open, and it's practically a damn hurricane-force rain. I roll my eyes. He always has to drive His point home. The hapless family gathers their stuff and hurry home.

I whistle for Black Shuck and jog toward the house. I hate water as much as I hate cold. I'm lucky it isn't snowing. The Boss has been known to play a strange trick or two to remind us He's in control. Of course, *I* always get the blame when something bad occurs. And the humans never take responsibility for *their* part. I don't know why He's so partial to them.

Ready to get out of my soaked shorts, I can't get in the house fast enough. I slam the door against the pounding rain and quickly peel off the disgusting wet garment. Black Shuck shakes the water from his thick black coat.

"Stop, ew!" Lili fusses.

"He's an animal, that's what they do," I point out.

"Not him! You, asshole!"

I pause, wet shorts in hand and grin. "Me? It isn't like you haven't seen it before." My wings expand and flap off the remaining water before folding and disappearing.

Lili throws a dishrag to me. "Cover up and go."

I raise one eyebrow, confused. "You're joking, right? Cover up with that?"

"Your ego is much larger than your other perceived attributes." She bites her lip but snickers.

I glare at her. That insult was uncalled for and *not* true. I'd call her an unflattering name, but I'm not stupid. I don't want to be castrated. She ignores my death stare and goes back to kneading her bread with more force than warranted. Flour dusts her cute face and red hair.

"I think you're working that bread a little too hard." I grin, pleased with my double entendre and wait for her reaction.

"I'm punching the air out of it and pretending it's your face. Now go get dressed," she says, not looking at me. "I'm not interested in what you have to offer."

Black Shuck looks at me with a silly grin on his demonic face. *Damn traitor.*

"I wasn't offering anything," I mumble, leaving. As I dress, I remind myself I'm trying the friend thing. After all, it was nice being able to reveal my wings and not freak someone out. Walking back into the kitchen, I find Lili's beautiful ass in the air. She's searching the bottom cabinet, swearing under her breath.

Down, boy. I'm talking to my dick, not my dog. My palm itches to smack that ass.

"Quit staring at my butt." She stands and throws the pan on the counter and faces me. Her confrontational stance is warranted. She knows me well. Time to disarm her with my charm and reassurances.

"What would you like to do today, *friend?*"

She plops the bread into the now-greased pan. "This has to rise and then bake, so I guess I'm stuck here. But you're free to go wreak havoc and hell elsewhere."

"Nah, it's boring doing it alone. That's my point in this friendship thing. I'm tired of being by myself."

"You know that I know you boink every human you can, right? Literally and figuratively."

"Not *every* one. And I'm turning over a new leaf. Why, I might even become The Boss's golden child once again."

She shakes her head, giggling. "I can't believe you managed to say that with a straight face."

I shrug and grin. "Me either. But it could happen. Come on, we'll get Blind Draeke to bake the bread and watch Black Shuck. Let's go pretend like we're humans. I know just the place. Pack an overnight bag."

"I'm not staying at some sleazy motel with you."

"When have I ever taken you to a sleazy motel? Okay, so the Last Drop Saloon in 1872 wasn't that great with the bedbugs, but come on, give me some credit."

"I don't know…"

"Please? We're on vacation — let's just relax and have fun."

"Where are we going?" Lili washes her hands and dries them.

"It's a surprise." I refrain from fist pumping my triumph. *She's going!*

"You have to give me a hint. How will I know what to pack?"

"Casual. It will be hot, thankfully. Shoes you can walk in, sunglasses, and sunscreen."

She narrows her eyes. "Bathing suit?"

"Sure, there's a pool at the *nice* hotel we'll be staying at, not that I'll partake, but you might enjoy a swim."

"Okay. Separate rooms."

"If you insist. But you can trust me."

"I do insist. And I'm smart. I don't trust you, never will."

"So be it. I'll go talk to Blind Draeke while you pack."

CHAPTER FIVE

The car slows to a stop, and I open my eyes. I must've been more exhausted than I realized. I sit up, feeling disoriented and vaguely uneasy. Looking out the window, my heart sinks. Of all the places to bring me, this is the last place on Earth I want to be. Maybe this is some kind of sick joke. I glance over at Luc as he parks the car. A wide grin spreads across his face.

"Surprise! How much more human can you get than Mouse Hell?"

I want to smack that goofy grin off his handsome face. I grip my purse strap and take a deep breath. I've never had a panic attack in my long life, but I think I'm having one now.

"I pulled some strings and booked a bungalow so we can pretend we're on some Polynesian island with a gazillion other sweaty, happy humans."

I swallow and force my dry mouth to work. "L-Luc?"

"Yes?" He pushes his sunglasses to the top of his head.

"Why don't we just go to a real island. You love Bora Bora."

"*Boring, boring.* And not what most humans can afford. This is the ultimate human experience!" He taps the steering wheel with his thumbs as he watches harried parents unloading suitcases as their excited children dance and scream.

My skin crawls.

"Don't worry, your non-existent virtue will be safe, there are two bedrooms and I'll even give you the master suite."

He steps out and the valet opens my door. I close my eyes for a moment, knowing I have two options. I can either sit in the car and pout or act like an adult. Pouting wins for the moment. I open my eyes to find Luc ducked down, peering at me.

"Come on, friend! Rides await us. I want to see the haunted house. I'll hold your hand if it's too *scary.*" His teasing, friendly grin eases my anxiety. I can do this; after all, I've play-acted like a human for years. I take his hand and step from the car. He tips the valet generously.

"So how do we get to the park?"

The employee offers, "You can take the monorail, bus, or boat."

"Boat?" Luc asks me.

Knowing he hates enclosed spaces, I weigh my options. "Bus sounds good to me."

Luc frowns, but we head over to catch the bus.

Twenty minutes later, I regret my decision. It's loud and full of excited children and their parents. I'm crammed next to Luc, and the heat from his body makes me even more uncomfortable. A bead of sweat dots his brow. The bus moves and excited shouts erupt around us. I want to vomit.

Luc wraps a protective arm around my shoulder, and I snuggle into his neck, trying to ignore the screaming kids. His seductive scent comforts me, which in itself is upsetting. He kisses my forehead.

"You okay?"

I shrug, not willing to share my feelings of inadequacy highlighted by the happy families around us.

"If we'd gone on the boat, we could've drowned a few of these obnoxious people and not be so confined," he whispers. I know he's only halfway joking. He's claustrophobic. I giggle, somewhat relishing the fact he's as uptight as I am.

"This was your idea, not mine. I would've been happy on a deserted island." *Happier. No kids.*

"Let's make the best of it. Come on, I know just the place."

After standing in line for what seemed like an eternity, we enter the theme park. Luc grabs my hand, pulling me toward a castle and then veers left. I'm practically jogging to keep up. We reach a gothic looking house, and I roll my eyes.

"Really? A haunted mansion?" I glare at the little brat stepping on my foot. In return, he smiles up at me with a sticky, toothless smile and offers me his cotton candy. I turn my back.

"I thought it would make us feel more at home. Remember the picnic we enjoyed at The Old Jewish Cemetery in Prague?" His grin widens.

"Shh." My toes curl and stomach clenches at the memory. We'd melted the snow around us with our hot, animalistic sex.

Standing in line with happy, noisy people, I find the excited chatter around us cloying. Luc rolls his eyes and whispers, "We're gonna need insulin by the end of the day."

"Or a gun," I hiss through clenched teeth.

The teenaged boy in front of us makes several loud, disparaging remarks about how lame the ride will be. I tend to agree with him. His parents tell him to hush, but he continues. At last, Luc and I get into our car and it jolts forward.

"Ready for some fun?" Luc whispers. "Watch this."

He disappears. I gasp, wondering what he's up to. The Boss will be pissed. We're supposed to blend in and act according to human restraints. Wings and disappearing aren't allowed. A blood-curdling scream from the teenager's car sends a chill down my spine. The maniacal laughter that follows makes me laugh. Luc swoops back into his seat.

"You're so bad," I say, giggling.

"Would you have me any other way?" He throws his arm around my shoulder in a casual manner. But my response is anything but relaxed. My skin tingles and my breathing hitches. Pressing my knees together, I shift away from him. He sighs and removes his arm.

The ride ends, and we meander through the park. Happy children bump into me, oblivious to my extreme distaste for them. I want to snarl like a feral cat. Instead, I withdraw into myself and stare at the ground, trying to ignore my surroundings. Luc nudges me and frowns.

"Are you sure you're okay?"

"Yes," I lie, and force a weak smile.

"Let's eat some junk food. I want to see what the fuss is all about." He tugs me toward a concession stand.

"You don't eat junk food?"

"Not if I can help it. I prefer three-Michelin-star dining." Typical of Luc, he orders for me without asking.

"What in the world are you two doing *here?*"

The voice from my past darkens my mood. I spin around to face my *ex* and his simpering wife.

Luc hands me a phallic looking thing on a stick.

Perplexed, I ask, "What is it?"

"It's a corn dog. Appropriate considering the company we're enduring." He turns his attention to Adam. "Scaring some of your progeny. It's been great fun. One kid nearly crapped in his pants at the spook house." Luc takes my hand and gives it a squeeze.

Eve frowns. "That's not very nice." Her perfect hair is swept into a perfect ponytail, and her perfect mouth forms a perfect pout.

"Here you go, precious." Luc hands her a candied apple and I laugh. He's always loved to irritate these two.

Adam grabs the confection and tosses it in the garbage. "Not funny."

I glance at Eve, who docilely stands there. I would have ripped him a new one, the jerk. I tear off a huge bite of the corn dog with my teeth and chew, licking my lips.

"Mmm." I pretend to enjoy it just to get under his skin.

Adam winces and turns to Eve. "What do you want to eat?"

Although Adam has *asked* Eve — unlike Luc — his officious tone sets my teeth on edge. Luc is an alpha male. Adam is just an ass.

"Whatever you want, I'm fine with," Eve murmurs in that subservient, docile manner that makes me clench my jaw.

I roll my eyes, and Luc smirks.

"They've got those mini cocktail wieners. She's probably used to minuscule meals," Luc offers.

"Oh, those sound good. I'm not really hungry. I'd be satisfied with that." The clueless twit smiles adoringly at Adam.

Luc turns to me, "I bet you'd like a foot-long." He smacks my ass, and his brows lift above his sunglasses.

"Let's go," Adam growls at Eve.

"Okay. Bye." She waves and dutifully follows Adam. I'm surprised she doesn't have to wear a back brace, the spineless, dumbass bitch.

"I want an ice cream cone!" an insufferable child beside me wails, the pitch high enough to make dogs run for cover. His mother indulgently placates him with a double scoop. Personally, I would've spanked him.

"Why on earth would anyone want ice cream?" Luc shudders and takes a bite from his corn dog. He frowns. "This is disgusting."

I laugh and nod. We toss them in the garbage.

Before we can escape, the kid doubles over and vomits on Luc's expensive shoes.

"Holy hell!" He whips off his sunglasses and glares at the sick little monster, flames flickering in his pupils. He's one pissed off angel. The youngster screams, terrified.

"Can we go now?" I tug on his hand and pass him some paper napkins. I'm so done with the crowds and especially the children. Any place would be better than here.

"You, madam, are the reason I'm under-employed," Luc snarls at the distraught mother as he wipes his shoes. "Uncontrolled children become undisciplined adults."

She begins screeching about jerks and intolerance as we walk away.

"Where to?" Luc asks.

My skin is crawling, and I just want to go home. "A shower?"

"I thought I got it all off. I'll just grab a bottle of water and rinse off my shoes if you want to stay. They have some rides that aren't too claustrophobic."

A woman bumps into me. The glare I level at her makes her step back.

"Sorry," she mumbles. Turning her attention to the baby in her arms, she smiles and coos nonsensical words to sooth the fretful baby.

Why do humans talk gibberish to infants? No wonder humans are developmentally behind. The newborn is wearing a ridiculous oversized pink bow on her head. Her outfit is pink. Her shoes are pink. Everything is so damn pink...and pretty. A yearning grabs my heart, and it feels like I'm having a heart attack. Tears sting and threaten to spill down my hot cheeks. I'm thankful my sunglasses hide my weakness.

Luc stops abruptly and faces me, cupping my cheeks. Using his thumbs, he moves my glasses to peer into my eyes. "What in Heaven's name is the matter with you?"

His uncharacteristic concern is my undoing. I grab his wrists and shake my head, afraid to speak.

He tenderly kisses my forehead. "Whatever it is, I'll make it better, my darling."

"Friends," I croak, wishing he could.

No one can. It's my curse.

"Well, *friend*, fuck this shit. I'm taking you back to the room. Something's been wrong with you all day."

The happiness on the hour-long bus ride is so sickening that I cling to Luc, burying my face in his arm. Typical, instead of whispering sweet nothings, he entertains me with the most ludicrous remarks about the humans surrounding us. His tactic works and de-escalates my impending panic attack.

After the longest damn day of my life, we finally arrive back at our room. To my surprise, he sweeps me off my feet and carries me in, kicking the door closed.

I don't resist. This has been inevitable since the day I arrived unannounced in his office. This is what we do, time after time. He'll be sweet, we'll have hot sex, and I'll fall a little more for him and mistakenly think things will be different. Then we'll have a huge fight and he'll leave.

I just need to encase my heart in barbed wire.

His lips brush my forehead. "I gotcha, babe."

Tomorrow…I'll encase it in barbed wire, tomorrow…

Something is off. I acknowledge I'm not the most sympathetic angel around. I leave *feelings* and *morality* to those do-gooders, Remi, Rafe, and Gabe. But Lili's worrying me. Her sun-kissed freckles stand out against her pale face, and she feels like a limp, fragile doll in my arms. Maybe I'll pamper her before fucking her brains out.

Yep, sounds like a viable plan…

Instead of throwing her on the bed and ripping her clothes off, I lower her gently. Before I can kiss her, one lone tear slips from under her sunglasses. I remove them, concerned and quite frankly, at a loss at what to do. She turns away from me, burying her face in the pillow.

"Please, just give me a minute," she whispers.

I've never seen my feisty girl like this. It's as if she's broken. A strange sensation occurs in my chest. *Is this what it feels like to have a human heart attack? Oh, hell, no. Not happening.* I'm the Prince of Darkness, Asshole Extraordinaire, King of the Douchebags. What she needs, and what I want, is good old-fashioned, mindless sex. Maybe with a little ass spanking and hair pulling thrown in for good measure. I kneel beside her, lean over...

Fuck.

Her lower lip is trembling, and she hides her face deeper in the pillow. All thoughts of seduction dissipate. *Okay, I lie. Not all.* I curl behind her, spooning her delightful ass. It's unfortunate we're both clothed. Shoving my baser needs aside, I pull her closer, and hold her.

"Stop." She shrugs me away.

I frown. *Stop, what? I'm not doing anything.* I kiss the back of her head, inhaling the exotic smell of her shampoo. The sun filtering through the window lights her hair, and it shimmers like spun copper.

"Please, just stop." Her voice sounds strangled.

"But, I'm being all nice and shit," I protest.

"I know. Do something asshole-like so I don't get my hopes up."

I nudge her behind. I'm as hard as a honeymoon dick. She giggles softly and swats me away.

"Better?"

"Much."

I inch closer, wrapping my arm around her waist as we spoon. She doesn't pull away, and after a few minutes, the tension eases from her body. I kiss my favorite freckle on her shoulder. She sighs and I close my eyes, relishing the familiarity of having Lili in my arms. A strange feeling settles over me.

Could this be happiness?

I don't admit it often, but despite being able to damn well have anything I want, nothing ever satisfies me. But right now, just holding her, I feel complete.

Or is this that strange phenomena humans call intimacy?

No. It can't be. I refuse and refute this thought. I'm never intimate, even when balls deep in someone. I admit, I came close with Jolene, but even she didn't crack through my self-imposed walls. Only the beautiful creature sleeping in my arms has ever come close...

And I fuck it up.

Every. Single. Time.

I'd say this time will be different, but I know better. I shove these absurd feelings or thoughts, whatever they are, back into their proverbial locked box. If I let it, despair could overwhelm me just thinking about all this. But I'm made of tougher stuff than that. I bury my face in her hair and hold her a little tighter. At least for now, it's all good.

CHAPTER SIX

My eyes snap open, and I find Lili's brilliant blue-green eyes staring at me. They're the color of the Caribbean Sea.

"I love watching you sleep," she whispers.

"So help me, if you took a photo and sent it to anyone, I'll spank your ass."

She giggles. "Promises, promises."

I run my finger down her cheek tracing the path her tear took. "You okay?"

Lili shrugs. "I might as well say *yes*. You can't help me. No one can. It's my own cross to bear."

I wince at the reference.

"Sorry." She leans in, pecks my lips and moves to get up.

My fingers interlace with hers, preventing her from leaving. "You know, friends don't shut each other out. Talk to me. What happened? Did I do something wrong, again? Was it seeing Adam and Eve? Want me to find him and do something reprehensible? Would that make you smile?"

She smiles, but it doesn't reach her eyes. "No, it was that *place*." She pulls away, wrapping her arms tight around her chest.

"Need a dose of insulin?" I tease, not really understanding what's wrong. I mean it was nauseatingly sweet and wholesome, but it wasn't that *bad*. Especially, when I scared the crap out of that kid.

She rolls to her back and stares at the ceiling.

I'm not known for my sensitivity. But she's in pain, and I find myself wanting to help. But I'll be blessed if I know what to say. What would that do-gooder Rafe do?

"Wanna fuck and get your mind off your problems?"

She glares at me and sighs.

Guess not. Shit.

"You're a pig. I'm going to shower. I'm hungry. And I mean for real food, not junk phallic-looking food."

I leer at her.

"And, definitely not *your* phallus." She flounces off the bed.

I fly off the bed and follow. Seeing Lili naked will improve my mood, and maybe I can improve hers.

"I could wash your back—"

The door slams in my face.

"Or, not," I mutter. Knowing her, she'll be in the bathroom awhile, simmering. I'm in deep shit, and we haven't even had sex yet. I consider contacting Rafe. He's known for being thoughtful and kind, but asking him for advice sticks in my craw. I could get in touch with Remi, but he's almost as clueless as I am. Instead, I leave her a note telling her where I'll be and wander outside to the pool for a beer.

As I order, someone sidles up beside me. "Buy me a drink, sailor?"

"Oh, for fuck's sake. What are *you* doing here? First Adam and Eve, now you. Is anyone left minding the Pearly Gates and playing the harp? Where's Gabe?" I glower at the platinum blonde bombshell standing beside me.

Madge laughs, not the least bit intimidated. I hate dealing with angels. Raking my eyes down her well-endowed form, I'm disappointed to find she's wearing a rather demure, one-piece red swimsuit. Mary Magdalene usually dresses a little more provocatively.

"Gabe's not here. I'm with Him." She nods toward the pool.

I pay for my beer, turn around, and damn near drop it. The Boss is reclining in the sun, dressed in shorts and a Hawaiian-print shirt. His white beard flutters, and He waves at some kids playing Marco Polo. He looks like fuckin' Santa on vacation.

Clouds instantly cover the bright sunlight and He's frowning, probably because of my language. *Can my damn day get any worse?*

He motions me over.

Why, yes, it can.

Saying no isn't an option. It never really is. He says jump, you're supposed to reply, *"How high?"* I down my beer and motion for another, girding my loins, so to speak. The last time we had a face-to-face conversation, things didn't go so well. I haven't been allowed back home since. I look to Madge for help, but she's too busy flirting with the bartender. I saunter over and collapse on the reclining beach chair beside Him.

"Samael! Oh wait, you prefer to be called Luc, don't you?"

"Yes, Sir."

I put my sunglasses on. Being in His presence is like staring at the sun.

"What are You doing here?" I search my mind, looking for any deficits in my job.

Wars ✓

Humans behaving badly ✓

Climate change ✓

Violence ✓

Reality TV ✓

"Don't be redundant. Wars, humans behaving badly, and violence all go hand-in-hand," He corrects. "And not all reality television is bad. I get a kick out of that show where the humans run around naked in the jungle. Makes Me think of good times, back in the day when Adam and Eve were running around cavorting…"

A stray beach ball bounces toward us, and He throws it back to the abhorrent brats playing in the pool.

"Quit worrying. You're doing a fine job." He stands. "Come walk with Me. This conversation should be done in private."

I frown and follow Him. "What are You doing here?" He pauses, and I add a belated, "Sir."

He stops under some palm trees at the edge of the property. "It's Sunday. I'm resting. Why are *you* here? This is no place for you."

He's right. *He's always right, dammit.*

He shakes His head in warning. He doesn't like cussing.

"I, uh…" *Crap. How do I admit to Him that I wanted to make someone happy?*

"How is Lilith? Like you, she doesn't stay in contact much."

Of course, He knows she's here. I shrug, not really knowing. "She's okay."

One bushy eyebrow lifts.

Defeated, I admit, "Miserable and I don't know why. I mean look at this place. Happiness drips from the fake façade. Everyone's happy here."

"Are *you* happy?"

The wind rustles through the palm leaves above us. I know He isn't really asking about my current frame of mind.

I weigh my words. "I — I have my moments, I guess."

"You chose this life," He reminds me.

I feel like that dumb cartoon coyote who always seems to run into an anvil. "You're kidding me. I *chose* this life?" Heat flushes my face as I struggle to contain my wings. "*You* chose this life for me. Why? Answer me! Because I questioned Your authority? I merely suggested some policy and procedure changes that could have been made to improve the running of Your day-to-day operation. You can't bear to have anyone go against You. You think You're the Almighty — okay, never mind, You *are*. But, You'd rather have those damn mealy-mouthed yes-angels who bow and scrape to Your every whim —"

The wind picks up and His beard whips. Trees bend and shade umbrellas topple as folks scramble to grab tables and chairs. *Oh, shit.*

"The delivery would've been better if you'd used your Jack Nicholson impersonation," He replies with a bemused smile.

The gale dies down, but my temper still simmers.

"You never listen to me!" I clench my teeth so hard my jaw hurts.

"Funny, I say the same thing about *you*." He strokes His beard and pulls at His bottom lip.

"Why can't I go home?" I blurt.

It's the question that's plagued me for eons. Not that I'd want to stay, but it's the thought of being forbidden to do something. I don't like the word *no*.

He crosses His arms. "Luc, you are my son."

"Really, Darth Vader?" I don't check the eye roll this time. "Go on, tell me how important I am."

He laughs. It's deep and robust, and the palms rustle from the impact. "I know you better than you think I do. You don't like being constrained by rules. I understand this; therefore, you live amongst the humans enjoying freedom. But all freedom has a price. My question for you is this: Is freedom worth it?"

"Why am I held to a different set of rules? Remiel is by no means perfect, but he gets to go home. Your precious humans are despicable and do atrocious things, and yet they're welcomed with open arms. Why me? Why do You hate *me?* Why am I being punished?"

He stares at me for a full minute. Nervous and twitchy, I pace, taking deep breaths to calm down. But I don't regret one damn word. I'm tired of being His whipping boy. Of course, He knows this. He knows everything. I stop and raise my chin, ever defiant, ready for the lecture, or learning lesson, whatever the hell He's calling them these days.

"Perhaps you need to change your perspective."

I throw my hands up and punch the air. "I should've known You'd twist this back to being *my* fault." I sneer.

I've never been able to talk to Him. We butt heads like mountain goats, always have, always will. Even with my sunglasses on, the brightness of His countenance burns my retinas. I drop my gaze.

"I don't think you realize the depth of My love. It's immeasurable. *Even for you.* Do you honestly think I'd trust just anyone to do your job?"

I open and shut my mouth. It's one of the few times in my long life I'm speechless. His words have moved me more than I want to admit. I look away, refusing to meet His gaze. Standing beside the pool, I see Lili talking to Madge. A large hat shields my girl's face. I like her aqua halter dress; it enhances her pale skin and fiery hair. It also makes her tits look great.

"Ahem." He sighs.

Dammit. I've got to be more careful; you can't hide anything from Him. The girls hug and Madge leaves with the bartender. Lili wipes her eyes under her sunglasses.

My heart gives a strange lurch. I need to find out what's wrong and see what I can do to help.

"Are we done?" I ask.

The Boss sighs. "Yes. If you change your mind and want to abide by My rules, you know how to reach Me."

"Yeah, right. Don't hold Your breath, Old Man." I move to make a hasty retreat before He changes His mind and decides to impart more words of wisdom. I'm worried about Lili…

"And Luc?"

I turn back and face Him, careful to keep my face neutral.

He nods toward the beautiful angel sitting beside the pool, dangling her feet in the water. Her shoulders sag as she watches the kids paddling in the water.

"She needs you. And you need her." He hesitates as if He wants to say more, but thankfully doesn't.

I give Him a curt nod and nonchalantly make my way toward her. Maybe I should've asked Him for advice, because I don't have a clue what's wrong, or what to do. But that's not how I roll. I'll play it by ear.

And pray I don't fuck it up.

Again.

Every female, and a few males, stop what they're doing and watch as Luc approaches. He's beautiful, charismatic, and he knows it. Behind him, The Boss waves before walking away. I nod an acknowledgment, both curious and nervous. What's He's doing here? Did Luc get in trouble for scaring that obnoxious teen?

I put my game face on and stand. I'm leaving and Luc's going to be pissed. I was planning to say good-bye and just disappear, but seeing The Boss has scratched that idea. He gets upset when we don't play by His rules on Earth. I guess I'll have to pay a driver. Shoulders squared, I face my Achilles heel. To my surprise, Luc brushes a kiss on my cheek.

"Feel better? Mmm, you smell good enough to eat," he teases.

"I'm fine and it's sunscreen, idiot."

"Ha! Any male worth his salt knows your words mean you're not fine. Were you crying when you were talking to Madge?"

"Crying? Um, no. Suntan lotion stung my eyes, that's all," I lie, giving him a reassuring smile.

He stares at me longer than is polite, but nods, accepting my answer. I'm not sure if I deserve an Academy Award or if he's biding his time.

"Ready to eat?"

"Eat?" I blink.

"Earlier, before your shower, you said you were hungry. Your wish is my command. What are you in the mood for?" He laces his fingers with mine as we walk toward the room.

No smart remark about how long it took me to get ready.

No moves to have sex.

It's like being in a parallel universe. Or having amnesia.

"I, uh, I'm going…I mean, I need to go home. I have a job to do, remember? I'm basically going to have to ghost write your memoirs." My stomach sinks. *Oh, crap.*

I stop and grab his arm. "Is that why The Boss was here? Is He upset about your book? Are we in more trouble than usual?" Unlike Luc, I try to fly under the radar where He's concerned. If Luc has dragged me into something, I'm really going to be upset. The last thing I need is Him on my case.

Luc snickers. "No, He's taking the day off. That Sunday 'day of rest' bullshit of His. What do you mean you're going home? We just got here. I thought we were on vacation. There's no hurry on the book. And I'm not convinced it's *that* bad."

He hugs my shoulder like we're pals and kisses my temple. Again, it isn't sexual. His actions are confusing the hell out of me.

Luc's face lights up, and he walks backward in front of me. "Hey, I have an idea. Let's go eat at the faux castle and pretend like we're back dining with old Louis and Marie Antoinette. We'll even eat cake in remembrance!"

"You have such a warped sense of humor." My overwrought nerves are making me anxious. I don't think I can continue this charade for much longer. I need to go home and be alone.

"It's part of my charm and one of the many reasons you love me."

A couple walks by pushing a stroller. Against my better judgement, I turn and the baby smiles at me. Suddenly, I can't breathe. It's like being hit by a sledgehammer in the chest. My vision blurs and I stumble. Luc catches me. I bury my face in his shirt and cling to him.

"I have you, love. I don't know what's wrong, but I've got your back."

His strong arms steady me. A need to connect with someone, even him—especially him—overcomes me. I clasp his neck and kiss him. He hesitates a mere second before reciprocating. My hat flies off, but I don't care.

I need him.

I want him.

Dammit, *I love him.*

Once again, he sweeps me off my feet, literally and figuratively.

"I can walk." I trail kisses across his scruffy jaw.

"Hell no, I'm not letting you go."

He manages to get the door open and kicks it shut. In record time we've shed our clothes, our hands and mouths greedy for each other. He mutters filthy words in my ears, and his wings flutter behind him as he pins me to the back of the door.

He forces my legs apart and finds me hot and needy for him.

"You're fuckin' mine," he growls. "I own you, do you understand?"

He plunges deep. I'm more than ready for him, it feels wonderful. I bite his shoulder. He yelps with pleasure and fire burns in his eyes.

"You're wrong. I own you, and you're mine," I gasp between his hammering strokes.

His fiery wings expand, and the power goes out with a huge *pop.* My wings cushion my back as he drives in to me, relentless in his onslaught. My red feathers float around us, and the smell of burning feathers permeates the air. He isn't making love; he's fucking me. And it's exactly what I want and need. My mind empties of the pain I've been harboring. In this moment, I'm living and feeling. It's primal and renewing. The temperature in the room rises to that of Death Valley in July, and smoke fills the air.

"Sprinklers," I whisper.

He grunts an acknowledgment and his wings retract, his pace slows and he walks me into the bedroom. I nip his earlobe, and he smacks my ass, hard. I moan and dig my nails into his shoulders. His smile is wicked and flames leap in his pupils. I hungrily kiss him, our tongues dancing, teasing, and tasting. Running my fingers through his mussed hair, I tug and smile. To my surprise, he collapses on the bed with me on top. After his teeth tug my nipples to the point of pain, his greedy hands cup my breasts and I settle into my rhythm. Closing my eyes, my head falls back. This feels so right, even though I know it's so wrong.

He grunts and meets me stroke by stroke, thrusting deep. Tomorrow there will be marks left on me from his ironclad grip, but I don't care. He sits up and grasps the back of my neck. The momentum picks up and I whimper.

"Not yet," he hisses. The air is heavy with the sounds and scent of our coupling. I scream his name as we both climax. Our bodies are slick with sweat, our breathing ragged as we reach the pinnacle of heaven on earth. He falls back on the bed, bringing me with him. We're still connected and it's more than physical. As I spiral back to the here and how, his heart pounds under my ear and I giggle.

"What's so funny?"

"You *do* have a heart. The rumors are wrong."

He chuckles. My labored breathing calms and Luc's heart slows, now in sync with mine. I feel limp and the buoyancy from my orgasm is gone as reality descends like a lead weight. I raise my head and his face blurs. In an instant, we've reversed positions.

"Thank you," he whispers, pushing my damp hair from my face.

"For?" I blink back my tears.

"Not calling out The Boss's name when you orgasmed. It's annoying as fuck when humans do it."

I laugh through my tears. "You're such an ass."

"I know. But it made you smile." He kisses my forehead and nuzzles my neck. "Tell me what's wrong, love."

I hesitate before speaking. I've carried this pain for so long…*Can I do this?* He strokes my hair and my defenses crumble.

"Do you ever long for something you know you can't have?"

"Nope," he answers a little too quickly. "Life is full of disappointment. You know that."

"But it's so unfair. And the fact we're immortal, makes it worse." I don't hold back on my bitterness. I hate feeling this weak and vulnerable. I've hidden this side of me from everyone.

"What are you talking about? Being immortal is the shit. We're forever young! What do you want? You name it. I'll get it for you."

"You can't give it to me, no one can." I move to get up, but he catches my hand.

"Look at me."

His overbearing bossiness pushes me over the edge. I yank my hand from his, and hop up, clenching my fists.

"A baby!" I shout. "I want a baby!"

One corner of his mouth lifts before his mouth flat lines. He looks shell-shocked. "Seriously?"

I swallow the lump clogging my throat and nod, blinking away my unshed tears.

"You're shitting me. That's not possible."

"Thank you for pointing that out, Captain Obvious. I should've known better than to confide in you." I flounce into the bathroom and slam the door. That's it. I don't care if I get in trouble with The Man Upstairs, I'm showering and going home. I've just revealed my greatest weakness to the one who can, and will, use it to destroy me the next time we fight.

The water is scalding hot, and I scrub my body, wanting rid of any reminder of Luc. The door opens and he steps in. For spite, I turn the hot water off. Cold water hits him full blast.

"Argh!" he yelps through blue lips as steam floats off his bedraggled wings.

My teeth are chattering, but it's worth it. Maybe he'll leave.

"Dammit." He grabs me, pins me to the wall and switches the water to steaming hot.

I wiggle my wrists, but I'm unable to break his hold. He stares at me, and I lower my eyes, not wanting him to witness my vulnerability, not to mention my humiliation. Luc releases my wrists and cups my face, kissing me tenderly. My silent tears mingle with the water trekking down my face.

"I'm sorry, Lili. Truly sorry," he whispers.

His quiet acknowledgment of my pain is my undoing. The dam breaks loose, and I cling to him, sobbing. And to my surprise, he doesn't tease, or make an inappropriate move.

He holds me and comforts me.

I gulp air like a drowning victim, knowing I'm in dangerous water. This is the angel I fell in love with. But this side of Luc never lasts, and I pull away needing to distant myself from him. Emotionally, I'm not ready for him to leave me. And leave me, he will. I must protect this last tiny piece of my broken, battered heart.

"When did you decide you wanted kids?" Hands on his lean hips, he stares at the drain in the shower as if it holds the answer to his questions.

I don't answer, unsure if this is a rhetorical question, or if he wants a real answer.

I swallow nervously. "When I became pregnant."

"Pregnant?" Disbelief pulls his brows together.

"I've miscarried, twice."

"Twice? But how is that even possible?" His voice sounds clipped as he soaps up and rinses. The visibility in the bathroom now resembles a steam bath.

"It happened a long time ago. Back before medical advances. I guess as science moved forward, my ability to conceive lessened. Maybe it's angel menopause?" I follow the weak joke with a hollow laugh.

Luc turns off the water and wraps me in a towel. I can't read his face. I'm not sure I'd want to.

"Why didn't you tell me?" Flames blaze in his pupils. "Some friend," he mutters.

I don't answer. *What can I say?*

"Get dressed," he commands.

Too emotionally spent to argue, I pull on my clothes and watch as he throws our belongings in the suitcases. Within thirty minutes, we're headed down the road. I close my eyes and let the motion of the car lull me to sleep.

CHAPTER SEVEN

I'm an excellent judge of character. It's what makes me good at my job. I know people's secret desires, their strengths and their weaknesses. But Lili's confession stunned me. *She's not human…*

A baby. No, babies.

My babies.

My gut tells me they were mine. And I'm not sure how I feel about the news. I glance over at her. She's sound asleep, her arms wrapped protectively around her stomach, her forehead resting against the window.

I envision a little red-headed girl with freckles, and the road blurs. I rub my eyes. What in Heaven's name is wrong with me?

Fuck protocol. I step on the gas and blink, the road disappears.

Three seconds later, I pull into Lili's driveway. Torrential rain hits the windshield and lightning arcs behind the bent palm trees. The Old Man isn't happy with me. *So, what else is new?* A boom of thunder shakes the car. Lili stirs, blinks, and glances at the clock.

"We're home already?" She frowns. "You always have to push His buttons, don't you?" Yawning, her halter dress stretches across those luscious tits.

"Don't worry about it. He expects it." I fight the wind to open my car door. The gale howls and our clothes are soaked in seconds. My independent girl scampers up the steps without my help. Leaving the suitcases, I run after her. The power is out, so I snap my fingers. The candles scattered throughout the living room flicker to life.

"Thanks. I'm just going to change out of these wet clothes and call it a night."

She stares at her feet and clicks her thumbnails. Her wet, red wings droop.

"Mine, are, uh, in the car."

I don't relish the thought of going back out in the mini hurricane and sigh. As pissed as He is, I might get struck by lightning. Besides, I don't mind being naked.

Lili leaves and return in minute holding a terry cloth robe. "Here."

I cross my arms. "You're fucking kidding me."

She shrugs. "Stay wet for all I care."

"It's lavender…and *fluffy*."

Walking by me, she pats my cheek. I witness the first smile she's cracked since Mouse Hell. "It will bring out the blue of your eyes."

She closes the door to her bedroom, and I hear drawers opening and closing. In my room, I strip and ruffle my feathers to get the excess water off. I'd go get Black Shuck from Blind Draeke's, but I don't want to get wet again. I hear her door open and shrug into the damn robe. I look ridiculous, but we need to talk.

Her damp hair is in a loose braid, and her sun-kissed face is bare of all makeup, making her freckles more prominent. Even dressed in pajama pants and a sloppy T-shirt, she's sexy as hell. Her throat bobbles, and she's keeping a safe distance from me. But it's her emotional distance that disturbs me even more. *What do I do?* I need to know and decide to pursue the truth.

"Why didn't you ever tell me you were pregnant? They were mine, weren't they?" *Please say no.*

She nods and runs her hand across the back of the couch, not making eye contact. Outside, the wind chimes clang as the wind whips around the house with a sorrowful groan.

"Both times I found out after we broke up and you were gone. Besides, what could you have done?" Her sorrow-filled eyes meet mine.

"I don't know."

Lili folds herself onto the couch, and I sit at the opposite end. I should do something, but I'll be blessed if I know what.

"Tell me something." Her eyes appear luminous with her unshed tears. "Have you ever wanted kids?"

I feel like I've just been kicked in the balls. It's a trick question. One of those horrible, damned-if-you-do, damned-if-you-don't questions for which there is no right answer. I'm fucked regardless, so choose to answer truthfully.

"No." I manage to suppress the shudder.

"There's your answer." She sighs.

"That's not fair!" I immediately regret shouting, but I'm pissed.

I had a right to know. This feels like a betrayal. I stand and pace, catching a glimpse of myself in a mirror over the mantle. I look ridiculous in the fuzzy robe. My fiery wings expand in ratio to my growing irritation. I'm spoiling for a fight.

"My work isn't exactly conducive to fatherhood. What happens when I arrive for *Bring Your Dad to School Day* and they ask what my job is?

"Hi, I'm Luc DeVille, and I'm here to instill jealousy, self-doubt and a sense of self-entitlement in your miserable little lives. Afterward, I'll give you a one-way ticket to Hell. Thanks for having me. Any questions?"

She rises from the couch and flames flicker in her eyes. "There was no kindergarten back then. And this is precisely why I wouldn't have involved you. You don't understand commitment. You don't understand love. You're a shallow, narcissistic, selfish bastard who doesn't deserve children." Sweat pours down her red face and damp curls escape her loose braid, framing her face. The heat in the room is that of a sauna.

Rage consumes me. Not because of her character assessment. I am all those things. But, *I don't deserve children?* Why not? This fight is going to be the mother-fucking-doozy of all the fights we've ever had. Emotions I'm not used to dealing with rise to the top, threatening to boil over. If I don't get out of here, I'm going to burn this damn place down.

I storm back to my room. The heat of my fury has dried my clothes, and I step into my pants. I'm beyond pissed. I'm fucking ballistic. *How dare she?*

I head toward the beach, slamming the door so hard something crashes behind me. The storm has passed, but the air remains heavy and sticky. Jogging past Blind Draeke's, I smell his tobacco. He must be on his porch smoking. I'm in no mood for company and don't stop. Black Shuck bounds toward me with a happy bark. I scratch his ears and he dances, wanting to play, but I'm too angry to play with him. Together, we run along the beach. I'd like to take off and fly to get rid of this excess energy, but can't risk it.

An hour later, exhausted, I stop, hands on my knees to catch my breath. The wind still whips and my limbs feel like lead. Moonlight emerges from behind a cloud and shimmers across the rhythmically crashing surf. Despite my distaste of water, I find the sound strangely soothing. A safe distance from the water, I sink to the sand and watch my dumb dog chase the waves.

Staring at the infinite stars, I listen to the give and pull of the tide. *Water.* It's life and associated with cleansing. I hate the stuff, but here on Earth it's a necessity. Without it, everything would die. Humans are even protected by it *in utero.* An image of a Lili with a rounded belly flashes through my mind. She'd be gorgeous pregnant. And from there my mind wanders to a redheaded toddler building a sandcastle and giggling.

Me, a father?

Impossible. And yet…

I sit up clutching my chest. I've been accused of being heartless. I even prided myself on being callous and ruthless. But this pain in my chest is real. I dash the moisture off my face. *Damn salt air.* This is insane. It can't be real. We're not human…Maybe it's just The Boss fucking with me. I could see Him asking Lili to help "teach me a lesson."

As a matter of fact, I bet that's exactly what this is. *She's putting Judas to shame.* How could she do this to me? Is it payback for me being inattentive for centuries at a time? I have a fucking job! Convinced I'm being punked by the Almighty, I leap to my feet and whistle for my hound. I'm going to give His cohort in crime a piece of my mind before I leave. I race toward the house, wings blazing and fully expanded. If it makes Him mad, it will be a bonus. Sure enough, it starts pouring before I reach the back door.

Lili's asleep on the couch, her arms wrapped around a pillow. Her nose is red, and a lone tear lingers on her pale lashes. My anger dissipates and my wings fold. Deep in my gut I *know.* This is real.

And my girl is hurting, and not in a hot, raunchy sex kind of way. This is deep, mind-shattering, soul-depleting anguish. The kind that might lessen but never goes away.

I drop to my knees. I can't even remember the last time I was in this position. Leaning forward, I stroke her hair and kiss her damp cheek, tasting the saltiness.

"I'm sorry," she whispers, keeping her eyes closed. Another tear escapes, followed by another.

"For?" I wrap her braid around my fist.

"I don't really think you're shallow."

I teasingly tug her hair. "But I'm a selfish, narcissistic bastard?"

We're skirting the issue at hand, and we both know it.

"Well yeah," she replies matter-of-factly with a small smile.

"Damn straight." I pull her from the couch and hold her in my lap. "I'm sorry, my love."

"You're wet," she mumbles.

For once, I don't care. The only thing I do care about is Lili. Her soft tears become a keening and I hold her tighter. She's mourning what could never be. It's the sound of a wounded soul and it rips through my already battered heart, connecting with my sorrow.

Life is painful and full of disappointment. We both know this, but this is perhaps the first time we've truly *experienced* it.

"Why? Why me?" she wails.

I have no answer for her. There is no answer except why not you? No one is exempt from pain. Unfortunately, here on Earth it's part of life and serves to highlight the good times. I continue to rock her, murmuring soothing sounds into her hair.

After thirty minutes, she's spent. Her heart-wrenching sobs have dwindled to quiet sniffles. I'm still at a loss about what I can do for her. I've never been one to ask for help, and I'm not starting now. There must be something I can do to fix this. I have everything in this world at my power.

Digging in my pocket, I offer her my handkerchief. Lame, but it's a first step. The torrential rain outside eases and the lights flicker but remain out. I glare at the ceiling. The generator hums, but we never bothered to turn the lights on.

Give me a break, Sir. I'm new at this side of the business.

She dabs her eyes and smiles. "How quaint. Oh look, you even have your initials on it. You do know that no one in this century carries a handkerchief anymore, right?"

I chuckle against her hair. "Call me old school."

"Old school?"

Her broadening smile encourages me, and I leap to my feet, determined to make her laugh. She has this adorable snort sometimes when she's really tickled. Setting the beat, I rap 2Pac's "Old School," complete with hand gestures. By the time I finish, the tears on her face are from laughing. No snorting, but it's a start.

"I hope you don't plan to pursue this as a part time job. You suck."

"Hey, trash-talker, don't be throwing shade on Smooth Luc D. And yeah, I've been known to suck. Want me to demonstrate *that* talent?" I lick my lips and give her a corny pelvic thrust and leer.

She shakes her head. "You're pathetic."

I pull her to her feet and cup her face. Pain still lurks in the depth of her eyes. Eyes I could drown in. "I am." I kiss her forehead. "I don't know what else to say or to do."

It occurs to me this is probably the most honest statement I've ever made to her. And she deserves so much more.

"I think I want to go home."

"We're at home." Dread clenches my gut. *She can't leave me.*

"I mean, *home.*"

"Home as in Heaven?"

She shrugs. "I'm lonely. Seeing Adam and Eve and all of their progeny just heightened my awareness of what I'm missing."

My wings expand with my frustration and fold with my growing guilt. I don't respond. I can't fix this and it's frustrating. And it's something more…Goddamn these *feelings.* Feelings are for weak angels and humans. Not *me*…The only Being to ever see me vulnerable is The Boss, and I swore it would never happen again.

This weakness is despicable. Why am I feeling guilty? I've never felt guilt over any damn thing in my long life.

Deep down I know it isn't guilt.

But her pain affects me. *Or is it my pain?*

I turn away and hang my head, confused.

Luc turns his back on me. The momentary relief his impromptu, silly rap brought me is gone. My heart feels like lead sinking in a sea of grief. What did I expect? It hurts, but it's just what I needed: a reality check. It's time to wake up and realize this is a toxic relationship. He's never going to give me what I need.

I'm not talking about children; I mean *all* of him. His love, his hate, his despair, his joy…And great sex just isn't worth the pain of this emotional baggage.

My lady parts offer a weak protest. *Okay, I can't lie. It's the best sex, ever.*

But a superficial relationship is no longer enough. I want more and deserve more. I take a deep breath. I can do this. We've been round and round for eons. It's time to break the cycle.

Standing tall, I keep my voice quiet, but firm. "I'd like to be alone. I think it's time you left."

His fiery wings flap once and disappear. Silent, he leans against the fireplace mantle, his head on his arm. I bite my lip. This isn't the response I expected. *Where's the argument? The flash of temper? The sarcastic, hurtful comments?* Something is wrong. I move to his side and ruffle his feathers. Slowly, he lifts his head. Instead of the flames that usually flicker there, his eyes are bright…with unshed tears? He blinks and the flames return. *Did I imagine it?*

"I…Of course." His jaw clenches. He appears lost.

I frown, never having seen him like this.

Black Shuck whimpers and nudges Luc. It isn't my imagination. Even his hound from hell knows.

Luc is in pain.

His despair illuminates the darkness of my own grief. *I'm not alone.* And neither is he. Whether he realizes it or not, he needs me as much as I need him. Like me, he's broken.

I just called him pathetic. The word derives its root from the Greek term *páthos* meaning *suffering, feeling.* He is indeed suffering, and I doubt he's ever experienced it before. Even when cast out of Heaven, he celebrated.

"Luc?"

No flames flicker in the depths of his pupils. No wicked smirk lingers. He stands straighter, and his face goes blank. He's shutting down, his walls are going back up.

"Luc," I say again, more firmly this time. I move toward him, but he steps back, his hand raised to block me from getting too close. That's always been his problem. He doesn't let anyone in; there's always this unspoken boundary.

"Let me in." I mean physically and emotionally, and I push into his personal space, a little unsure how I'll be received.

His throat bobbles. "You would've been a spectacular mother. I can't imagine what our kids would've been like, though. Demons, I guess, with fiery tempers." His attempt at humor is yet another defense mechanism. It ranks up there after his sarcasm.

"Hellions for sure. Beautiful little hellions." I bite my lip, refusing to cry any more.

Luc falls to his knees. Startled, I cradle him against my empty womb. His arms snake around my waist and his shoulders shake as he buries his face in my stomach. There are no tears, but his grief is palpable. Warm hands creep under my top, pulling me closer. With his eyes closed, he reverently kisses my stomach where two of our children once resided. I stroke his blond hair. His silence speaks more than words. I sink in front of him and grasp his face.

My sweet fallen angel.

My beautiful soul mate.

My love.

This is the pattern of our relationship. I know he's going to infuriate me and there will be times I'll regret being involved with him. But we're angels cut from the same fabric. We're much more alike than we are different. Yes, we fight. Yes, we hate. But we also love. We're passionate loners who manage to connect when needed. And now that he knows about our children, we're bound together forever in our loss.

No one comes close to Luc and no one ever will. In my long life, I've had many lovers. In that respect, I've been no "angel" and neither has he. But they were nothing but a diversion, pale substitutions for him.

We're destined to be together.

Growling, he pulls my top off and kisses each breast. Looking up, he bites my nipple and tugs. Passion once again flickers in his eyes.

My head rolls back and my nails dig into his shoulders. This isn't going to be gentle love making. It's going to be raw, it's going to be hot, and nasty. He rips my pajama pants off and flips me to my knees. Grabbing my hair, he twists and yanks as he delivers a loud slap across my bottom. He sheds his jeans and teases my entrance from behind.

Pulling my hair, he snaps, "What do you want?"

"You."

His fingers acknowledge the truth of my words. I'm wet and ready for him.

"Damn straight you do." The temperature in the room soars. He plunges deep and growls, "I'm going to make you forget everything else. *I will be enough for you*; do you hear me?"

When I pause a second, another slap burns my ass cheek. He grips my hips and pulls back slowly. I hold my breath, waiting for him to slam into me. I'm ready for the aggressive, bruising sex he's known for. Instead, he leans forward and trails kisses across my shoulders.

Thrown by his gentleness, I shiver, unsure what to expect. I need more. I need to forget the past and so does he. Nothing annihilates the pain of being alone like coupling with your other half. I wiggle, encouraging him. He pulls out and rubs my stinging butt. I hold my breath, waiting for his next move. Craning my neck, I find him staring at me. The only way to describe his look is contemplative. My anxiety level skyrockets and my knuckles whiten.

He blows his mussed hair off his forehead. "I want to try something…different."

I attempt to swallow, but my mouth is as dry as the Sahara Desert. I like rough sex. He does, too. But is he wanting to push me further than I'm willing to go? Apprehension heightens my awareness of him.

He's a predator, I'm his prey.

A slow smile spreads across his handsome face. Sand still clings to his body. The soft lamplight accents the ripples of his abs and cut of his biceps. The flames flickering in his eyes mirror the slow expanse of his fiery wings. He's devastatingly beautiful.

He's also unpredictable. And dangerous. And I want him more than ever.

Luc stands and lifts me into his arms.

"Where are we going?" I kiss his jaw, my heart racing with anticipation mixed with a healthy dose of fear.

"Hush." He kicks my bedroom door closed. Black Shuck whimpers his displeasure at being locked out. Lowering me to the bed, Luc kisses my forehead. "Move off this bed, and you'll be sorry. Understand?"

Of course, my first inclination is to jump up. I hate being told what to do. But something in his demeanor keeps me rooted to the bed.

I nod.

Luc treads to the bathroom and I hear the shower. I frown, knowing he detests water…

Despite his instructions, I turn the bedside lamp on. A moment later, he steps into the bedroom, naked.

"Tsk, tsk. You moved, didn't you?" He stalks toward me. "I'm surprised you didn't light the candle. I know how you love hot wax…"

I nod, scooting until my back hits the headboard. I have no clue what he has in store for me. He snaps his fingers, and we're plunged into darkness. The bed dips, and I hold my breath, gripping the duvet as he moves over me. The candles scattered around the room flicker to life and his fiery wings slowly expand behind him. He crawls closer and closer. Looming over me, his head drops and he places a gentle kiss on my lips.

"Breathe. The rumors are grossly exaggerated. I'll happily provide you with *la petite mort,* but I'm not into necrophilia."

Air whooshes between my teeth and I giggle. His wings fold, and he lies down with his head on my shoulder. His hand lazily strokes my flat stomach.

"Boy or girl?"

My gut clenches at his soft inquiry, but he continues caressing me until I relax.

"Boy the first time. Girl the second."

He sighs. I run my fingers through his damp hair.

"When?" he asks.

"First time during the First Crusade. You were working long hours stirring up hatred. The second time was in 1521 when you were busy goading Martin Luther."

"He overreacted; there was no reason to throw an inkwell at me."

Luc remains silent and I don't push. *What is there left to say?*

He rolls to his back and pulls me close. "I'm not father material."

"I know." My disappointment leaks through my words.

He kisses my forehead. "But I'll say it again. You'd be an amazing mom."

"Thank you."

He props up on one hand. "I could talk to The Boss. Maybe there's something He could do. Would you be willing to surrender your angel card and privileges? And get old and die? From what I've witnessed, it can be unpleasant at times."

I've thought about this. *A lot.* "I don't know. Would you?"

"I could lie and tell you yes. Like we discussed earlier, life is difficult, more so for humans…especially those who don't have hope. I'm a creature of habit. I like to play hard, take the road of least resistance. I know my strengths and limitations. My job keeps me busy. And I value my freedom. Parenthood isn't for me."

"And if I became human? Where would that leave us?"

He doesn't answer as the back of his fingers grazes my cheek. I swallow and look away.

"I don't know." His hand smooths the hair from face. "I kind of doubt our paths would cross much. Unless you're a heinous mother. Which I know wouldn't happen. And there would probably be another guy or girl in your life."

"I can't imagine my life without you," I confess.

"I feel the same way. I know I piss you off on a regular basis. But I also know you'll always be there when I return. I've taken you for granted, and I'm sorry for that."

He rolls on top of me and kisses me. His warm mouth encourages mine to open and let him explore. I sigh, but this time with contentment. He smiles as he kisses me and nips my bottom lip.

"Like I said earlier, I want to try something different."

I bite my lip. My emotions are all over the place. His words sound final. Is this it? The last good-bye? He takes my hands and places them over my head. "Don't move," he whispers.

Soft kisses trail across my collar bone and down my breast. He releases my hands, but I keep them above my head. His warm hands knead, tease and tug my nipples and his hot mouth follows, exploring lower and lower. He spreads my legs and kisses behind my knees before placing both legs on his shoulders. I squeak when he nips the tender spot on my thigh. My flesh tingles with anticipation as his lips draw closer and closer to the spot that begs for his attention.

I lower one hand and ruffle his hair. He chuckles.

"That's my girl. I wondered how long you'd remain obedient."

"Ass." I tug his hair. "Quit teasing."

"That's me! And the Devil is in the detail." He waggles his brows.

I groan, first at his silly quip and then because he finally takes me in his mouth, sucking, licking, teasing me unmercifully. When his fingers enter, and find the magic spot, I shatter. Usually when this happens, he follows by taking me swiftly, roughly. He'll be relentless in his onslaught until I orgasm again. But this time he leaves a burning trail of kisses back up my body. He kisses my forehead and slowly enters me.

He smiles down at me. "I love you, Lilith. I've loved you for ages and always will. I'm never more alive, than when I'm with you. Don't tell Him, but you bring out the good in me. You're the light in my darkness, and I wish I could give you what you want, I truly do. If you decide to go human, I'll support your decision. I want you happy. What I'm saying is, I love you enough to let you go."

His arms cage me as he moves within. He's not fucking me, he's making love to me. Gently, sweetly.

I run my fingers down his cheek, my thumb brushing his mouth. He kisses my palm.

"Is this good-bye?"

"We always say good-bye." He kisses me. "And we always say hello." He grasps my hands and holds them beside my head. His rhythm picks up and I wrap my legs around his waist. Closing my eyes, I give in to the experience that is Luc. He's right. We part ways, but we always find our way back to one another. Like the tide, we will ebb and flow, but our relationship will always be constant.

This time when I go over the edge, he's right there with me.

CHAPTER EIGHT

It's afternoon when I roll over and discover Luc gone. The bed is cold and empty, much like my life now. I thought he'd at least wait until I was awake to leave. Sure enough, his clothes and hound are gone, too. I shower and dress in my favorite red dress and grab my wrap. Despite it being the middle of summer, a fierce breeze blows off the gulf, whipping the sea oats and palm trees. Dark clouds loom on the horizon, moving toward the shore.

I slowly make my way down to the beach. It's deserted, magnifying my feelings of loneliness. I'm confused. And angry. Usually when he leaves, it's in a fit of temper. But last night he'd been loving and gentle...

I stare at the ocean and look deep within myself. I'm far from perfect. All my life I've pretended to be in control. But it's been a lie. I've lived for approval, first from The Boss, then Adam, and finally Luc. I need to put actions behind my words and become a strong, independent angel. I must forge my own destiny and make my own happiness.

Having a baby isn't going to solve my problems. It's time I grew up and made peace with who I am and what I am. I deserve happiness. And I must find it on my own. The thought is liberating, the plan attainable.

Laughing, I twirl in the sand, my scarf whipping behind me. If it wasn't forbidden, I'd unfold my wings, take off, and soar. My scarf billows and seems to lengthen.

A bark from down the beach stops me. I brush my hair out of my eyes. Black Shuck bounds toward me, occasionally getting side-tracked by a crab and the waves beating the shore. Where is Luc? I can't believe he'd leave his hound behind with Blind Draeke.

I jump and giggle when warm arms wrap around my waist. His chin nuzzles my neck.

"'Bout time you woke up, sleepy head."

I turn my neck to look up at him and smile. "I thought you'd left without saying good-bye. I just decided to stand on my own and take charge of my own happiness. Now you've ruined my feminist resolve."

He turns me around but keeps his arms around me. "Lili, I meant what I said last night. I love you. Our lives will always intermingle. The Boss called, and I have to go. My bags are packed, but I was waiting until you woke up so I could say good-bye. I'm sorry, love, but you know my job requires me to travel. We aren't human. Hell, I'm not even your typical angel…"

"I know." I hug him tight.

I smile, happy. This time feels different. *It is different.* He's leav-ing, but we aren't fighting. I'm at peace with how we are. "I love you, my rebel without a cause."

"Of course you do. What's not to love? And what do you mean without a cause? I'm the Marquis of Mayhem. My job is important. He couldn't function without me—"

Thunder booms, the heavens open and torrential rain soaks us. I giggle and kiss his wet face.

He lifts me over his shoulder and smacks my ass. "He always has to prove His point. I hate the damn rain." Whistling for his dog, he marches back toward the house. "After we dry off, and before I leave, I'll show you a few tricks another Marquis shared with me…"

EPILOGUE

"Ms. Nix? Someone is here to see you. He doesn't have an appointment, but he insists."

I look up from my report and frown. "I have a staff meeting in a half an hour. Tell him I'm busy and to please schedule an appointment."

"I did. He's quite insistent." She blushes and I raise an eyebrow. This isn't like Kelley, my all-business assistant.

"He's um, kind of hot."

The door bursts open, and Luc strides in wearing a black suit and red tie. "I won't take much time. I was in the neighborhood and thought I'd stop by."

I roll my eyes. This poverty-stricken area is hardly his "neighborhood." Kelley snickers and leaves, closing the door. I stand and walk around the desk, curious why he's here.

He looks around my office and goes to my favorite wall. It's covered with photos of babies and children interspersed with drawings and thank you notes. It's my pride and joy.

"What happened to your editing/publishing business?"

"I quit years ago. If you ever bothered to stay in touch, you'd know that. I now work in a field I'm passionate about. What did you decide about your book? I haven't seen it on any bestseller lists."

"I sold out. I opted to not publish in exchange for a vacation. The Boss made me an offer I couldn't refuse. I'm thinking the beach sounds nice. I have a *friend* with a beautiful house." He winks.

Hands clasped behind his back, he strolls by the wall, looking at my pictures. Suddenly, he stops and leans in closer. He points at the photo. "No way. Is that you? Smiling? In Mouse Hell?"

"Yes."

"Nice ears." He chuckles and spins around to face me.

I cross my arms and smile, resisting the urge to jump in his arms. He's been gone fifteen human years this time. No way I'm letting him off this easy.

"My guest room is available. Where have you been? You could've texted, Skyped, or phoned."

"Here and there, raising hell, stirring fires. *Pfft,* I've been gone longer without contact. That's like fifteen minutes in angel time. Tell me about this place."

He's right about the angel and human time difference, but still, he's terrible at communicating.

"We operate on human time here."

"So, you missed me?" If his feathers were out, he'd be preening.

"Not at all."

He smirks.

"Yes, dammit, I've missed you. This is a clinic for underprivileged women and children. We provide prenatal care and pediatric care." I cock my head and smile.

He's acting all nonchalant, but he knows, *I know.*

"Lili's Little Angels wouldn't be possible without my anonymous benefactor."

He grins. "Sounds like a decent human being."

"Who said it was a human being? And he's far from decent. He's downright indecent."

He moves like a sleek panther ready to pounce. Flames flicker in the depths of those captivating blue eyes. I giggle and back up until my butt hits my desk.

"Damn straight. And I've missed you too, love. Let me show you how much." He whispers everything he plans to do to me. Outside the sun is shining but it's pouring down rain.

"The devil's beating his wife." I bite my lip, anticipating his next move.

He bends me over my desk and smacks my ass. "Indeed. And she's going to enjoy the hell out of it."

I buzz Kelley and tell her to hold all my calls and cancel my appointments.

The End

ACKNOWLEDGMENTS

Special thanks and much love to Katherine Pace for editing this short story while preparing for her wedding! Thank you to Chantell Reid Photography for the beautiful cover photo of Wendy Hinkle. This photo captivated me and the first time I saw it, I knew it was my Lili. And a huge thank you to Coreen Montagna for turning the beautiful photo into a stunning cover. And for always making the insides of my books as pretty as the outside. You're the best.

To my ever-patient hubby who "holds the fort" as I cuss at the computer and my daughter, parents and sister for being my cheer-leaders.

ABOUT THE AUTHOR

During the day, Nancee works as a nurse/counselor in the field of addiction to support her coffee and reading habit. Nights are spent writing paranormal and contemporary romances with a serrated edge. Authors are her rock stars, and she's been known to stalk a few for an autograph, but not in a scary, Stephen King way. Her husband swears her To-Be-Read list on her e-reader qualifies her as a certifiable book hoarder. Always looking to try something new, she dreams of being an extra in a Bollywood film, or a tattoo artist. (Her lack of rhythm and artistic ability may put a damper on both of these dreams.)

Website: nanceecain.com
Blog: nanceecain.com/blog
Facebook: facebook.com/NanceeCainAuthor
FB Street Team: facebook.com/groups/Cain.Raisers
Twitter: twitter.com/Nancee_Cain
Pinterest: pinterest.com/nanceecain
Goodreads: goodreads.com/Nancee_Cain
Instagram: @nanceecain
Newsletter: eepurl.com/bhFwvD
YouTube: bit.ly/2xsU6Ad

If you enjoyed *Loving Lili*, check out *Tempting Jo*

Forbidden love is hell...

Confident and quirky, Jo Sanford thinks her boss is God's gift to women—and she couldn't be further from the truth. Devilishly handsome, Luc DeVille will stop at nothing to lure his administrative assistant right into his arms—and bed.

Over Rafe Goodman's dead body...

Rafe, refuses to sit by and watch as Luc tries to win the heart of the woman he's always protected. After all, Rafe is her guardian angel.

But Jo's infatuated with her HOT boss. Caught in the middle of a battle between good and evil, Jo finds the closer she gets to the fire, the hotter it burns.

When love battles lust, Heaven and Hell collide.

Tempting Jo is available now at:
Amazon
Barnes & Noble
iBooks
Kobo

Continue reading for a sample from the first two chapters!

Tempting Jo
Chapter One

"Hey, Rafe. You've got a cleanup on aisle E."

"Not my problemo." I don't bother looking up from the mystery I'm reading. "I'm off duty."

"The Boss wants to see you."

Slamming the book closed, I glare at Remiel. "Why didn't you say that in the first place? Jerk."

He laughs and falls in stride with me as I rush toward the office.

"How's Evangeline?" I ask him, preening my wings and catching a white feather that flies loose. He's either been moping or raising hell with his pranks since returning home last year.

"She's okay." Remiel shrugs, his black feathers rustling. "Taking life by the balls." He hesitates and sighs. "I miss her like crazy."

I nod, sympathizing. My brother risked everything when he fell in love with the girl he was sent to rescue. In my opinion, it was stupid, but he's always been a renegade. Still, he was careless about hiding his true nature. That put all of us at risk. He should have kept his focus on the job. We've all had to do it. Even me.

Personally, I'm a by-the-book kind of angel. Rules bring order. I'm known as the problem-solver. The Boss calls on me when it's something big because of my ability to assimilate into any situation. My favorite was the time I convinced Anne of Cleves that her head would look better on her shoulders. The look of surprise on Henry's face when she agreed to the annulment was priceless. It's been a while since The Boss has requested my services, though. I don't count my recent stint spying on Remiel as a job. That was more for sport, and also unsuccessful because he refused to listen to reason.

"So what's going on? Who's in trouble?" I ask.

"I dunno. I'm just the messenger. Gabe was busy and couldn't deliver the summons. I wouldn't keep the Old Man waiting, though. He's already pretty upset. He hasn't been able to crack level 666 on that candy game He plays on His phone."

"That's bizarre. I mean if anyone could, He could."

"You know how He is. He likes to experience what frustrates the humans." Remiel hurries past me, grabbing Peter's keys. He takes off flying as Peter raises Cain in hot pursuit.

I pause, straightening my wings before knocking on the huge wooden door. The knock isn't needed; it's just a courtesy. He knows I'm here.

"Come in, Raphael."

The door swings open on silent hinges. His bright presence burns like the sun, illuminating the stained glass windows behind Him. Classical musical plays in the background. The Boss's wooly eyebrows are knitted together as He stares at His phone.

He pulls on His lower lip. "Quite annoying. More so than that silly Rubik's Cube from a while back." He looks up, and the blinding light causes me to blink and squint. He motions with His phone. "Have you tried this game?"

"No, Sir. I find it ridiculous and a complete waste of time."

One bushy brow rises a fraction of an inch.

"I mean, it's just not for *me*, Sir."

"You really need to learn to have fun, son. You're much too serious."

Heat flushes my face, and a knot forms in my stomach. There's no way to describe the feeling when you disappoint Him. Despair bleeds into your soul, infusing every molecule of your being. Another long minute passes as He finishes His game — unsuccessfully, judging by His scowl.

"Sorry, Sir. I'll, uh, catch a game of Go Fish with Peter later."

"How can that be fun? We all know that old rascal cheats."

"Yes, Sir." I remain standing at attention.

He sighs and rolls His eyes. "At ease, son. I'm not upset with you, Raphael. I just wish you'd lighten up. It's okay to have fun. I know you and Mary Magdalene had a good time when I sent you after Remiel."

He thinks we had fun? This surprises me. I'm still kicking myself for the way things went down. "We failed in our mission, Sir. Remiel fell in love with Evangeline. He should have left and let me deal with it. I take complete responsibility—"

"Stop." His voice rumbles like thunder. He looks up from the phone, His attention now focused solely on me. I don't like it—not one bit—when He's perturbed.

My feathers stand on end, and my wings flap despite my attempt to hold myself together. Remiel listened to my advice about as well as Marie Antoinette did. I told her she'd regret the cake comment, and I counseled Remi to let Evangeline go. In my opinion, The Boss was a bit too easy on him. And we all know what happened to Marie.

"Do you really want to go there?" He asks softly.

Having an omniscient boss sucks at times. "No, Sir. I'm sorry."

His face softens. "Relax. I've already told you, I'm not angry, nor am I disappointed in you. When was the last time you had a vacation?" He walks around to lean against the desk, facing me.

"Um, let's see…I think it was nineteen fifty-three. Peter and I attended Queen Elizabeth's coronation. Peter enjoyed the pageantry." Personally, I'd been bored to tears and found *I Love Lucy* more entertaining.

"Peter does love the smells and bells. He can be a bit pompous. And that's one of my favorite shows, too. Lucy always gets in trouble, but her heart is in the right place. Good heavens, you're way overdue for some off time, my dear boy."

"I don't need a vacation, Sir. I'm content working."

He studies me, and I lower my eyes for a second under the intensity of His stare.

"*Content?*"

"Yes, Sir. Perfectly content." My wings ruffle, and I shift on my heels.

He raises His brows and folds His arms. "Do you think that's My goal for you? To *just* be content?"

His question throws me. *Is this a trick?* "Uh, yes?" I swallow and add, "Sir."

"You need to live a little, Raphael. Everyone needs time off to relax. Even *I* took the seventh day to—how do they say it now?—chillax? However, there's a problem you need to handle first."

I contain my smirk and stand tall, ready for my assignment. "Yes, Sir." I hope this will be something interesting—like espionage.

The Boss picks up a file folder and scans the contents. "Ah, yes, here it is. That sweet Jolene is getting in a little over her head."

Stunned, I blurt, "Who?" Surely I didn't hear Him right. I do my best to hide my growing trepidation. I'm not prepared to see Jolene again…I was hoping for something a little less *personally* dangerous.

"You heard me. Jolene Sanford. You're her guardian angel. Brown hair, hazel eyes, quiet but feisty young woman. You spent quite a bit of time with her when she was growing up and having a rough go of things with her folks. She seems like a nice girl. How could it possibly be dangerous for you? You always adhere to the rules."

"When I left, she was fine and on the right track. I can't imagine her in a predicament, Sir. She's a little, er, *boring*." I hope He buys my attempt at deflecting as I try to remember how old she is in human years now. Twenty-five?

"Should be a perfect fit." He smiles widely and winks.

Busted.

"Just check on her. After you're sure she isn't headed in the wrong direction, take a week off and enjoy yourself." He cuts me off with a raise of His hand before I can protest. "That's all. Go. And relax; act like a human."

That last remark irritates me. Remiel caused a lot of chaos last year doing precisely that. I'm nothing like him. *I* take my job *seriously*.

"Raphael?"

"Sir?"

"Have fun." He walks back around His desk and picks up the phone, grumbling under His breath about the complexity of the stupid game.

I leave, wondering what the hell Jolene has gotten into. Truth is, she is anything but boring. The one kiss we shared is ingrained in my soul. It's one of the reasons I hastened home when she turned fifteen.

Tempting Jo
Chapter Two

"**F**riday."

Over the intercom, the clipped voice sounds tinged with annoyance, sending a shiver down my spine. It's too early to decide if that's in a good or a bad way. But probably bad. I'm two minutes late.

My name is Jo Friday...

No, not really. It's Jolene Loretta Sanford. To my misfortune, my mother's a huge country music fan. My family and friends call me Jo. My boss calls me Friday, because he can't remember my name. I'm not important enough for him to notice, even though I've been his administrative assistant for six weeks now.

But this will change. He *will* notice me, because I'm attentive to details. That's what makes me good at my job.

Administrative assistant. It's actually just a fancy title for flunky or whipping girl. My co-workers refer to my job as the *admin ass*, because they think only a dumbass would take the job. Mr. DeVille goes through admin asses like my daddy used to go through beer before he went to the pen: fast and furiously.

Now that I think about it, *whipping girl* might not be so bad. Being spanked by Mr. DeVille is currently one of my favorite late-night fantasies. Regrettably, this isn't likely to happen any time soon. I'm not exactly his type. I don't look like Barbie, and although I sound like a redneck, my IQ is above that of a drunken gnat. However, I'm taking steps to improve myself, and as I've mentioned, I'm determined to make him notice me. I know this obsession with my boss isn't healthy, but it is what it is. He's the most fascinating man I've ever met. And he has ambition, like me. He owns this business! He's not like the losers back home who are satisfied living and dying in the same boring town, doing the same boring jobs their daddies did.

"Friday, I'm counting. One…"

The dreaded countdown. No one has ever survived past three and kept their job. That's why I'm his fifteenth assistant in three months. This isn't like me. I'm usually competent and avoid the counting altogether, but this morning I overslept. My second job and night school are kicking my admin ass. My brother thinks I've taken on too much, but I can handle it. I know this opportunity presented itself for a reason. How many jobs come with a place to live built in? And working so much helps pay for school, so in that respect it's made my life easier.

Picking up the phone, I hit the intercom button and respond using my best professional voice. "Yes, sir?" Hard as I try, I can't quite curtail the drawl that clings to my words like honey on a Sunday morning biscuit.

"You're late. Has some catastrophic event occurred? A hangnail, perhaps? A run in your stockings?" His dripping sarcasm reminds me of wet quilts on a clothesline, heavy and unflappable.

I grin, picturing steam coming out of his ears like a cartoon character. "No, sir." I glance at my unpolished, bitten nails and comfy black pants. *Note to self: buy stockings and garter belt, get manicure.* "I apologize for my tardiness, sir. It won't happen again."

As my mother would say, sugar wouldn't melt in my mouth. She has all kinds of cliché sayings like this. She dishes them out like fried chicken at a Baptist funeral. Thinking about my mother firms my resolve to improve myself. I refuse to end up like Crimson Bryant Sanford: living in a trailer, miserable and strung out on prescription meds because of some SOB who treats her like dog poop.

I want a man who treats me like a beautiful princess in public and a naughty schoolgirl in the bedroom. And I know just the man for me: *Mr. Lucius DeVille.*

Far from stupid, I know right now I'm so far out of Mr. DeVille's league, I couldn't make it into the dugout, much less out on the field. He's high cotton, and I'm just plain ol' polyester. But this will change, or I'll darn well die trying. I'm saving any extra money that doesn't go for living expenses and school. Someday I'll have enough for some lipo and fake tits. In the meantime I could at least use a new wardrobe. Until then, I'll work on my education and lose the hick accent. A sweet, refined, soft Southern drawl would be okay. Men seem to like that.

Through the phone line, I hear Mr. DeVille's fingers drumming on his desk, and cold fear courses through my veins. *Shoot, the countdown started again. Please don't let him have made it to three!*

"Two…"

The frostiness in his voice makes me break out in a cold sweat. I *need* this job to pay for school. I *want* this job to be close to the object of my obsession.

"Sorry, sir. I'm here." *Phew.*

"Where are the reports I asked for yesterday?"

Although I can't pinpoint his accent, Mr. DeVille's brusque manner is that of a damn Yankee. Yes, that's one word, and it isn't considered cussing when referring to those of the Northern persuasion who have moved south and stayed. No one knows where he's from or why he bought this little company three months ago. All of his employees fear him, except me and my best friend, Rafe Goodman.

Okay, maybe I'm just a *tad* afraid of my employer.

Just after I got this job, I was surprised when Rafe showed up to interview one day—that's another reason I know this is meant to be. We hadn't seen each other in years, yet we reconnected like it had been just a few weeks. Rafe was my best friend growing up, and he gets me like no one else. We share a love of corny sitcoms and movies. It's great to have him back in my life, especially here at work.

"On your desk, sir." I let out the breath I've been holding. I'm on top of things. My middle name should be Efficient. Smiling, I place a single pink rose and a white feather in the vase on my desk. Rafe leaves them for me every Monday. Of course, he leaves the other five women in the office a rose, too. But mine is always pink and always accompanied by a white feather. I pull out today's paper and tuck away the coupons for myself. I don't consider it stealing since I used to dig them out of his trashcan anyway.

"And my coffee?" Although cool, Mr. Deville's voice sends a warm thrill all the way down my body, curling my toes.

Shoot, I have to get my act together. "I will gallivant to serve you, sir." *Gallivant* is today's word on my Word-A-Day calendar. Rafe gave it to me as part of my Christmas present last month. *To roam about in search of pleasure.* I'm not quite sure I've used the word correctly, but I'm too tired to care at the moment. I ignore my boss's growl of frustration. I'm used to it.

I yank open my desk drawer, reapply my deodorant, and run to the break room. Rounding the corner I find Rafe holding court with the twins I've nicknamed Tweedle Ditz and Tweedle Dumb. I doubt they got their jobs based on their typing skills.

Everyone loves Rafe. When I was six, I ran away from home and got lost in the woods. He found me and became my best friend. The man knows more about me than most, including the details of my unhappy childhood. But he's a little older than I am, and we drifted apart after he left for college. By then I was living with my brother, so my home life had improved. I wanted to stay in touch, but it was like he'd disappeared off the face of the planet.

The most popular guy in the office, Rafe has an amazing ability to carry on a conversation about absolutely anything and sound like he knows what he's talking about. Today he's discussing fashion trends on the red carpet. Yesterday he was talking football stats. He's like one of those lizards that can change color to blend into his environment. Back home in our small town, he wore jeans and T-shirts. He taught me how to throw a ball and bait a fishing line, even though I hated doing it. Here in Birmingham he dresses like an upper-crust New York businessman and wheels and deals like a high roller. The man was born to be a salesman, and his numbers reflect that. He's always number one on the board in the break room and could probably sell the Devil ice water in hell.

Tweedle Dumb rubs against him, purring like a feline in heat. Crossing my arms, I stare daggers at her until she leaves. To my credit, I refrain from making a gagging noise when she blows him a kiss. Tweedle Ditz tosses her hair and smirks. She and her sister would love to get their manicured claws in Rafe. Thankfully, he's too smart for that. He's constantly warning me not to get my honey where I get my money, and he seems to live by that rule. To say he doesn't approve of my obsession with Mr. DeVille is an understatement.

"If you need anything, you know where to find me," Tweedle Ditz simpers, straightening Rafe's tie.

"Sure thing. Thanks." Rafe turns his attention to me.

Dismissed, she leaves, her smile faltering. She glares at me on her way out the door.

I stop myself from sticking my tongue out at her. "I think I'll go vomit now."

"Jealous?" He winks at me and pours himself a cup of coffee.

I snort. "No. Except maybe of their fake boobs."

Rafe's intense gaze scans me from head to toe. He shakes his head. "Fake boobs are overrated. Good grief. What's up with your outfit? This isn't nineteen eighty-three, and you're not graceful enough to star in *Flashdance*. Didn't I buy you a new sweater for Christmas?"

I glance down at my worn black leggings adorned with white cat fur and my baggy, oatmeal-colored sweater. I look like a walking advertisement for the local thrift store. In contrast, dressed in black pants, an electric blue shirt, and a striped silk tie, Rafe looks like he just stepped out of the pages of *GQ*.

I roll my eyes. "Your brow's getting an old man furrow from frowning. The sweater is in the wash. Is this your not-so-subtle reminder that I still owe you a Christmas present?"

"Well, now that you mention it…" He grins, and it softens his critique, but he's right—I'm a hot mess.

My two arch nemeses are always dressed impeccably and are probably size zero despite their humongous fake boobs. I don't have money to spend on clothes. Prior to landing this job, I didn't care. *Comfortable and serviceable* was my motto; *cheap* was my standard. I've realized this too must change as I immerse myself in the study of all things Lucius DeVille. I've earmarked this week's paycheck for a trip to TJ Maxx, the poor girl's Saks.

"Thanks for the free fashion critique. Is my current ensemble a step up from when you asked me if I was wearing one of Sophia's sweaters from *The Golden Girls*?" I start a new pot of coffee. I wouldn't dare deliver anything less than fresh to the boss.

"If you say so." His raised eyebrow says otherwise. "Ludicrous the Devil sent you for coffee? What's the matter? Did he break a leg?"

"I don't mind doing this."

"He's a sexist tyrant." Rafe crosses his arms.

"Just stop. Don't *you* have a job to do?"

"I'm doing it."

"Standing around criticizing?"

"Protecting you."

"Oh, for heaven's sake. From what? I'm getting my boss a cup of coffee. He isn't going to throw it at me."

"I wouldn't put anything past him," Rafe counters.

"Mr. DeVille may be demanding, but he isn't evil."

"Trust me, he's evil incarnate. Play with fire, and you're bound to get burned."

I roll my eyes. "Don't you think you're being a little overdramatic?"

"Fine. Don't listen to sound advice." Rafe shoves away from the counter and storms back to his office.

I know he's not really mad. This is just how he gets. Sometimes he acts like I'm still six years old. When the coffee's done, I add three-fourths of a yellow packet of sweetener to Mr. Deville's cup. On the specific china plate he designated for his personal use, I place half a whole-wheat bagel with one tablespoon of light cream cheese. He eats the same thing every day. Once he takes notice of me, I plan to add a little variety to his life—starting with plenty of spice. On my way to his office, I pick up his mail and the paper from my desk. I've folded it so the headline is visible.

Mr. DeVille's on the phone when I enter. He doesn't spare me a glance as he rubs his forehead, barking orders at the hapless soul on the other end of the line. I place two aspirin on his breakfast plate, stealing a peek at the man I've shadowed for six weeks. Well, officially for six weeks. I guess Rafe's right; I'm kind of a stalker, but not the creepy killer kind. Even before I got the job as his assistant, I watched and studied him as I quietly cleaned his office while he worked late. Most people don't notice those who clean up after them, and Mr. DeVille is no exception. That's why I'm so good at this. I paid attention to what he likes.

Without stopping his conversation, he hands me a note with a woman's name and address written on it. One of my jobs is to send Mr. DeVille's thanks-for-the-sex flowers on Mondays. It really griped my butt the time I had to send matching bouquets to the twins. He doesn't care about any of these women, and it's always someone different. He can't seem to find what he's looking for.

I often fantasize about writing a snarky note to accompany the bouquets, such as: "I get lost in your cavernous depths of desire." I'm pretty sure it would fly over the recipients' empty heads. From what I've seen, Mr. DeVille's "dates" only speak in sighs, slurps, and two-syllable words. *Hey, there's an idea.* Maybe for Valentine's Day I'll have Mr. DeVille send his women a Word-A-Day calendar. They'll be half-price by then.

When I become his girlfriend, there won't be any need for these flowers. I'm not a casual sex kind of girl. And I definitely don't like to share. No, when he's mine, it will be for keeps.

Today Mr. DeVille's wearing my favorite gray suit with a lightly starched white shirt and lavender, gray, and black striped tie. Back home, no self-respecting man would wear a purple tie, but it looks spectacular on him. I like the way it sets off his ice blue eyes. Just looking at them makes my heart race. At times, I swear I can see flames flickering in them.

He's in need of a trim, and one strand of his blond hair has fallen out of place. I know for a fact he has an appointment with his barber after lunch. He has his hair trimmed every third Monday at exactly 1:15 p.m. I twist my fingers together to keep from brushing the stray lock from his forehead. I like his hair best on the morning of trim day. I'd love it even more mussed after a night of wild, freaky circus sex.

He hangs up the phone, and his lips press together when he realizes I'm still here. Just once I wish he'd look me in the eye.

"Anything else, sir?" *Me bent over your desk? Or a blow job? I'll even attempt to swallow…*

"No." He picks up a report, ignoring me.

I've just been dismissed without so much as a look or wave of acknowledgment. He never says thank you. I don't think the two words exist in his vocabulary. Hiding my disappointment, I leave quietly, closing the door behind me.

Someday he'll notice me.

The door closes, and I chuckle to myself. Jolene Sanford looks at me like I'm a damn piece of chocolate cake at a weight loss convention. Sometimes she licks that tempting, plump lower lip as she stares, making her appear ravenous. I make a note to research her family and see if there are any Donners lurking there.

I call her Friday because she's so damn efficient. And it keeps her at arm's length. I can't show my hand, yet.

Friday is pretty in an unassuming way, although she isn't at all confident about her looks. Her dark, wavy hair has a hint of auburn in it, and she usually has it pulled up in a ponytail or a bun. She needs very little makeup with her perfect complexion, and I like her natural look. Tall and charmingly awkward, she moves like a coltish tomboy, as if she's not quite comfortable in her own skin. Those golden hazel eyes with flecks of green are her prettiest feature. I like it when they flash with ire after one of my many unreasonable requests. She keeps a lid on it, but I know my assistant is full of piss and vinegar. It's her fiery nature that has started to intrigue me.

Her taste in clothes runs understated and casual, but I have to wonder why she doesn't own a damn lint brush. There's always white fur on her clothes. I'm not fond of animals as pets — the lone exception being my fiendish hound, Black Shuck.

I much prefer people as pets.

Though I haven't revealed it yet, Friday has most certainly captured my attention, and this cat-and-mouse game is proving quite entertaining. More so than I anticipated. The silly girl thinks she's in control. Little does she know, this whole scenario is part of a bigger plan.

I toss the aspirin in the garbage — now that I'm off the phone, my head feels fine — and down my perfect cup of coffee. Grabbing the files I need for the board meeting, I slip out the door, hoping she's at her desk. The office staff scurries to appear busy, like rats on a sinking ship. Do they really think I don't know they've been gossiping and checking their social media? I find Friday with her butt in the air, fiddling with her chair. I clench my fist to keep from smacking her admin ass as it wiggles in front of me. I clear my throat and wait for her to acknowledge my presence.

"Hang on. I've almost got this chair fixed so it'll quit lowering on its own. If that cheapskate would part with some money, maybe I'd get a chair that didn't sink like the *Titanic* every time I sit in it."

The noise in the office stops. It's as if her words hang suspended in the air, and it takes every bit of self-control I possess not to smirk.

Friday stops adjusting the chair and freezes, sucking in air like one of the hapless victims on that ill-fated ship. The clock on the wall ticks off time like a death knell.

"Oh, sho-ot." With her southern accent, the one-syllable word stretches into two.

She slowly stands, and her neck flushes pink, the color working its way to her hairline. Her eyes scan her co-workers in a desperate plea for help. None will be received. They may present themselves as human, but they're actually a bunch of slimy, self-serving invertebrates. It's why I hired them, of course. Only Raphael has any balls about him, and he isn't here. A full minute ticks by in silence, and not one of them offers her a lifeline.

Then Mr. Holier-Than-Thou rounds the corner and pauses, shooting me a death glare as Jolene fidgets in front of me.

"Friday." I keep my face blank, my tone even.

"S-Sir?" Her pupils dilate to the point it's hard to detect their hazel rim. If she doesn't breathe soon, I'm afraid I'll be forced to utilize my rusty CPR skills.

"Have lunch delivered promptly at eleven thirty to the board room, the standard order. Make sure you buzz me precisely at one for my appointment at the barber." I turn and walk away, determined not to smile at the relieved huff of air escaping her lips.

No one dares to look me in the face as I stride past. Out of the corner of my eye, I see one of the workers slip another a twenty. I'm sure it's for the numbers board circulating among the drones. They're betting on how long before I fire her.

That isn't going to happen. As a matter of fact, this is the first morning she's not been on top of her game. Perhaps I should get her a new chair, or at the very least, a lint brush. Not only is she the best damn assistant I've ever had, she's integral to the whole reason I'm here.

I square my shoulders, mentally preparing myself for my tiresome board of directors. A more apt description of our weekly conferences would be *bored* meetings. For the next hour and a half I'll contemplate either killing them in a slow, torturous manner, or a self-inflicted lobotomy.

Everyone thinks I'm a ruthless ballbreaker. They are correct. What they don't know is that I hate everything about this place. I couldn't care less if we're in the black or the red. I'm not a businessman. I'm on a mission, biding my time, toying with one of His favorites. My real job goes way beyond the scope of this petty office.

An hour later, the threat of snow thankfully cuts the board meeting short. Snow in the South is an interesting phenomenon. Just the hint of it has everyone rushing to the grocery store to buy milk and bread, which is asinine. If the power goes off, why would you open the refrigerator to get milk? And don't people usually have milk and bread in stock for normal days? Wouldn't it make more sense to buy condoms and liquor? This is Alabama. They don't get snow that lasts more than two or three days. It should be a party occasion, like Mardi Gras.

Looking up from my computer, I minimize the screen when I hear the timid knock on the door. Mrs. Cabot, the office manager, approaches my desk like a rabbit skirting around a hungry mountain lion. I've contemplated screaming *boo* just to watch her jump, but she's elderly, and I choose not to be responsible for giving her a heart attack. Too much damn paperwork involved. I make a mental note to have Friday schedule a CPR class for the office.

"Yes?" I raise an eyebrow and give her my patented annoyed look. I'd be lying if I said acting like an asshole was an act. The truth is, I *am* an asshole.

"M-Mr. D-DeVille, as you know, we are under a threat of ice and s-snow." She twists a tissue in her hands, blinking rapidly behind her thick glasses. Her corkscrew gray curls bounce with her nervousness.

"And?"

"Some of your employees live quite far away. S-Schools are being released early."

I sigh dramatically. "I suppose everyone wants to go home."

She nods, apparently relieved by my intuitiveness.

Elbows on my desk, I steeple my hands together and glare. "With pay?"

Her throat bobbles, and her face blanches to the color of paste. The shredded tissue scatters like the very snow she's scared of.

I heave another gargantuan sigh. "Very well." I motion her out the door.

"T-Thank you, sir," she snivels, reminding me of Bob Cratchit as she beats a hasty exit.

Just call me Ebenezer.

Tempting Jo is available now at:
Amazon
Barnes & Noble
iBooks
Kobo

pine bluff
series

For something different, you can also enjoy Nancee Cain's Contemporary Romances in the Pine Bluff Series. Each book has ties to the fictional small town of Pine Bluff, Alabama, a place where everyone knows your name and your business. Although you can read them as stand alones, characters weave in and out of other stories so you can catch up on your favorites.

The Resurrection of Dylan McAthie

NANCEE CAIN

The Resurrection of Dylan McAthie

AT SEVENTEEN, MUSIC LEGEND DYLAN MCATHIE RAN AWAY FROM his Alabama home to chase his dreams. Years later, he's forced to return — coming full circle to escape the nightmare his life has become. Hounded by paparazzi and plagued by the aftermath of personal and professional loss, Dylan craves some quiet anonymity so he can regroup and sort out what lies ahead.

Hired by his estranged brother, Jennifer Adams knows exactly who Dylan is. She grew up next door to his family and has followed his career. But the surly, overbearing man she's caring for as a private-duty nurse is far from the charming boy she remembers. Nevertheless, she's determined to be professional, do a good job — and not fail at her first time getting away from home.

As her patient heals, his demeanor softens, and their interactions grow less antagonistic. Soon their chemistry is undeniable — and inappropriate — leaving the inexperienced Jennifer thoroughly confused. Adding to the turmoil, scandal finds Dylan once again, threatening all the progress he's made and putting Jennifer at risk as collateral damage.

It's up to Dylan to fix what his fame has so easily broken and find a way to move forward with his life. But will his resurrection mean the death of any relationship with Jennifer?

Available on Amazon, Barnes & Noble, iBooks, and KOBO

The REDEMPTION of Emma Devine

NANCEE CAIN

The Redemption of Emma Devine

AFTER THE UPHEAVAL OF BEING DUMPED BY HIS GIRLFRIEND, DAVID Patterson leads a quiet life as a high school teacher in the small Southern town of Pine Bluff, Alabama. Soon to enroll in seminary, his dreams are within his grasp.

But a chance encounter with Emma Devine changes everything. She's on the run, desperate, and surviving by any means possible. His pastor's heart longs to help her—and the rest of him is rather intrigued as well.

His random act of kindness brings them together, but Emma makes an unfathomable decision—one that threatens to destroy two lives, though her intention is to save one.

Four years later, Emma returns, seeking redemption. But can David—whose dreams took a very different course after their last meeting—forgive her and risk losing everything?

Available on Amazon, Barnes & Noble, iBooks, and KOBO

www.ingramcontent.com/pod-product-compliance
Lightning Source LLC
Chambersburg PA
CBHW070805120626
46557CB00002B/718